WILD SOUL

KINGDOM OF WOLVES

C.R. JANE

MILA YOUNG

CONTENTS

DEDICATION

For all our readers who love the wild side of life...
get ready to enjoy the ride.

JOIN OUR READERS' GROUP

Stay up to date with C.R. Jane by joining her Facebook readers' group, C.R.'s Fated Realm. Ask questions, get first looks at new books/series, and have fun with other book lovers!

www.facebook.com/groups/C.R.FatedRealm

Join Mila Young's Wicked Readers Group to chat directly with Mila and other readers about her books, enter giveaways, and generally just have loads of fun!

www.facebook.com/groups/milayoungwickedreaders

KINGDOM OF WOLVES SERIES
FROM C.R. JANE AND MILA YOUNG

Wild Moon

Wild Heart

Wild Girl

Wild Love

Wild Soul

Wild Kiss

These stories are set in the Kingdom of Wolves shared world, but our Wild series will follow Rune's continuing story with her alphas.

WILD SOUL
REAL WOLVES BITE...

As soon as his teeth sunk into my neck...I was lost.

Just when I think I've found an answer to the hundreds of mysteries in my life, another appears.

This time, in the form of a vampire who seems to know secrets from my past...and who is desperate for my body and my soul.

My enemies are circling, looking for a way to break me apart and separate me from my two alphas. And their power seems to be growing.

We're determined to keep them away, but fate may have other plans.

My heart will always be Daxon and Wilder's, but what about my blood...

I'll do anything to keep them after everything we've been through.

But it's going to take a wild soul to do it.

Blinding Light
The Weekend

abcdefu
Gayle

Following the Sun
Super-Hi, Neeka

Let Somebody Go
Coldplay, Selena Gomez

Boyfriend
Dove Cameron

ABDEFGH I love you still
SongsforJacques

Middle of the Night
Elley Duhe

No One Can Fix Me
Frawley

10 Things I Hate About You
Leah Kate

ur just horny
Gayle

Don't Forget Me
Way Out West

Listen to the **Wild Soul Soundtrack** on Spotify

1

RUNE

After the first burst of pain as his fangs tore into my throat, I was ashamed to admit that pleasure took over. Ares let out a low moan as he sipped on my blood. I should have been struggling against him, but I was finding it impossible to move. I was aware of the room full of hungry vampires around us, their gazes cutting into my skin as they watched Ares jealously. But it was as if they weren't real, as if they were only in my imagination. There was only the feeling of wanting this for the rest of my life. I wanted to feel this good forever.

Ares abruptly dislodged his teeth from me, and I whined as my legs faltered. Before I could fall to the ground, Ares caught me. He pulled me into his body, nuzzling into my hair as one hand threaded around my waist, and the other wrapped around my neck, his thumb stroking my bleeding pulse point softly. The thrall began to fade, and my eyes widened as the fact that I was in deep shit came roaring back to me.

One of the vamps stepped forward, his hair a strawberry blond color, but an unnatural shade of it, almost like he'd taken blood and smeared it through his blond hair to create the effect. He was eyeing me like I was a rare steak dinner, and I found myself pushing back against Ares, like my body thought he would protect me even though he'd already shown he was a traitor.

"I'm next," the vamp growled, his eyes beginning to glow a brilliant shade of red. A low growl emanated from Ares's chest, rumbling against my back soothingly. "No one else is feeding from her tonight," he said casually, even as the whole room erupted into outraged roars.

"What the hell does that mean?" the vamp asked through gritted teeth, his sharp incisors lengthening as I watched. More than ever, I wished in that moment that I could call for my wolf. She would be able to handle the situation much better than I could. She'd tear everyone in this room apart.

At least I thought she would.

"Her blood's much too powerful to be spilled and used all up tonight. I need to think of a way to make it last. The kind of power she holds in her blood could solve all of our problems if we had it as a steady feeding source," Ares explained, his voice still so mild, like he was discussing the weather and not talking to a bloodthirsty, half-crazed vampire who was about to jump him.

"That's not what we agreed to," the vamp said before he lunged towards us. Before he could make it, Ares casually flicked the hand that had been wrapped around my throat, and the vamp was frozen in place, his eyes rolling to the back of his head and his body shaking as his blood started to drain from his nose, ears, and eyes. A startled gasp burst from my throat as I watched the macabre scene in front of me.

"Anyone else want to question my authority?" asked Ares.

The whole room had gone silent, their attention on the dying vamp in front of them. Or at least I thought he was dying. I wasn't up to date on vampire anatomy, but I was pretty sure that Ares was draining all of his blood out of him. Maybe the stake thing was real and he would need to be finished off with a stake in the heart after this, but he was going to be nothing but a dried-up corpse of a creature when this was finished, all the way dead or not. Ares showed no mercy; he didn't stop the bleeding until the vampire had fallen into the puddle of his own blood, splashing it around him, literally resembling a dried-out husk in a cornfield at the end of fall.

"Now, if no one else has any objections, I'm going to go upstairs and figure out how to make this best work for us," Ares announced, keeping his arm locked around my waist as he turned and shuffled me towards the set of stairs behind us. I had to admit, he had big balls. He was turning his back on a room full of predators. I could feel the palpable hate they were throwing at us as we walked away. We got to the base of the stairs, Ares threw me over his shoulder, and I grunted as his shoulder dug into my stomach.

I couldn't help but watch the room until everyone disappeared from sight. I was expecting at any moment for them to come after us, but no one took a step forward.

Once we got to the top of the stairs, there was a long hallway, but Ares made no move to put me down. He glided down it, and then another hallway until we got to a closed door at the end of it. He opened it swiftly and walked in, slamming it behind him and then twisting the door lock and then another lock at the top of the door—not that it would do much if they were really going to come after us.

Except Ares was still full of surprises apparently, because he muttered a spell and the locks both glowed red briefly before returning to their normal state.

"That will hold them off for at least a few minutes longer if they decide to be idiots and challenge me," Ares explained as he gently moved me off his shoulder and set me down on the ground. His hands moved up my body until he was cradling my face. His thumb stroked my skin as he gazed down at me... lovingly?

The intensity of his gaze was so much that it took me a second to snap back to reality. But when I did, I ripped my face from his hands and shuffled backwards across the room, keeping him in my sights while trying to get as far away from him as possible.

Ares didn't look angry at my retreat. He was still looking at me like I hung the moon. Like I was the altar that he wanted to worship on. What the hell was going on?

"So you're the villain after all," I finally said in a hoarse voice.

He cocked his head as if he was contemplating whether my definition fit him or not.

"I am the villain, but I'm not *your* villain. I'm never going to hurt you again." He sounded so believable...so sincere, that I'm sure anyone meeting him for the first time would be following him hook, line, and sinker. I obviously had just witnessed him charming my entire town with this façade, as well as me. There wasn't going to be a good enough explanation he could come up with to explain what he'd just done. Leading me to some kind of vampire lair, and drinking my blood while promising to feed me to them later? Unforgivable.

"I don't think there's anything you can say that would convince me otherwise," I told him, watching as he flinched from my words. I was getting major whiplash from the guy. I mean, the words that he'd said right before he'd ripped into my throat still echoed in my head and rang in my ears. "Before you..." I began, my words faltering at the memory... and the pleasure that had come afterwards.

"Before I bit you," he said nonchalantly, his eyes gleaming in satisfaction.

I waved my hands in the air awkwardly. "Yes, that. You called me 'your highness'. You said you'd been 'tracking me'. And then you said I was going to 'pay with my 'life'. And now you're trying to tell me you didn't mean any of that?"

He bit his lip, and I steadfastly ignored how sexy he looked doing it.

"That was before," he said, as if it should explain everything.

I sighed in frustration, some of my fear ebbing away. At least in this moment, he didn't seem like he was going to tear my throat out and drain my blood. "Before what?"

"Before I realized you were my blood match."

Blood match.

I didn't like the sound of that. It sounded...important.

"Blood match," I said slowly. "Am I supposed to know what that means?"

He shook his head gently, a fond smile on his face. Maybe he'd been possessed by someone as he bit into me. I mean, I definitely knew that that could happen. If vampires were real, body snatchers had to be real too. The way he was acting...it was just so different from the hate I'd seen in his gaze right before he'd pounced on me.

"It means that you're mine, and I'm yours. You're the

other half of my soul. My perfect girl. The one thing I never thought I'd get. Ever."

He took a step towards me, and I flinched. He immediately froze, conflicting emotions warring on his face.

"It sounds an awful lot like a fated mate kind of thing," I mused slowly, a million memories crashing down on me—none of them good. "And I've already had enough of that to fill a million lifetimes."

He shook his head again but didn't make any more effort to come towards me. "It's biologically impossible for me to hurt you once the blood match is recognized. It would be like hurting myself. There's no one in this world or any other world that could ever love you like I do."

"You sound insane," I spit. My heart and mind were rejecting the notion that fate would tie me to another person. The thing about Daxon and Wilder, who were hopefully freaking out right now, was that I was going to be able to choose them. While Miyu had been terrified of that idea, it brought me comfort. I'd never wanted to be in a situation again where the Moon Goddess could tell me I needed to be with someone. Fated mates weren't supposed to be able to hurt you either, but there I was, an example of how your world could literally end by the hands of someone the stars had fated for you.

The problem was, as much as my heart and mind were rejecting what he was saying in every way, there was a part of me...perhaps my soul, that recognized him. I pictured a cage in my mind, stuck that part of me inside, and slammed the door shut.

A thought occurred to me. "You've drunk my blood before though. And you were well on your way to trying to kill me. Why are you just now recognizing the match?" My hand went up to my neck which, I realized belatedly, was still trickling blood.

"Can I fix that for you?" Ares asked, his features pained as if he was hurting because I was hurting.

Which was fucking ridiculous. That was such a fated mate thing to do.

The mental cage I'd created rattled as whatever it was inside of me that felt bonded to him struggled to get out.

"Answer me first," I insisted, taking one last step back until I had nowhere to go and I was plastered against the wall.

He winced and looked away from me for a second before meeting my eyes once again. "I assume it has something to do with the fact that I didn't use venom with this bite, so your blood wasn't tainted and I was able to recognize it."

"What does your venom do?"

He looked guilty as fuck with my question. "It takes away the pain. You might feel a slight prick at first, but then nothing. I—wanted it to hurt when I bit into you today."

I shivered as I remembered the almost indescribable pain I'd experienced as he'd ripped into my throat and then the pleasure that had come afterwards. "Did you use the venom after you recognized the blood match? Is that why it felt so good?"

Ares's eyes lit up. "It felt good?" A brilliant smile flashed across his face, so stunning it almost took my breath away. "That's the blood bond then, because I never used any of the venom. Your body recognized me," he said smugly.

I rolled my eyes, and his smile dimmed. "Can I heal you yet?"

"How does that work?" I asked stubbornly, determined not to buy into the nice guy routine he was giving me.

"I can seal the wound by licking it. My saliva can heal it completely, you won't notice anything."

I bit my lip, staring at the floor as my hand went to my neck. It did hurt really fucking bad. I was surprised my neck was still there, honestly, and that the blood was just trickling out. It felt like he'd torn a hole in my neck.

"Please," he said hoarsely, an ache in his voice.

"Okay," I finally murmured after a long pause.

He walked towards me slowly like he was approaching a feral animal, and I felt feral in that moment. I obviously couldn't have a moment of fucking peace. If I wasn't being chased by my ex, haunted by ghosts, cursed by a fae, chased by beasts in the forest...I had to meet up with a crazy obsessed vampire.

Half the time I was still expecting to wake up and find out that everything that had happened since coming to Amarok was a dream. I still expected to wake up in Alaric's living room, serving him drinks.

Ares' nearness drove me out of my slight descent into madness. He was standing right in front of me, and honestly, he was so beautiful that it was difficult to stare at him. He had that glow to him, the same one that Daxon and Wilder had. A supernatural beauty that made them stand out from everyone around them, even other supernatural creatures.

The feelings I'd locked in my imaginary cage rattled again. Something inside of me wanted to lean towards him, wanted to feel him hold me in his arms.

Whatever goddess was responsible for this whole blood match thing needed to go to hell, quite honestly.

He leaned towards my neck, and I jumped. "What are you doing?" I yelped.

"I don't have a Stretch Armstrong tongue," he teased in

an almost whisper. "I do have to get a bit closer to do the whole licking thing."

"Right," I said, hating how breathy my voice sounded.

He leaned in, and I found myself holding my breath. Ares' warm tongue slid along my wound and my insides quivered…because it felt far too fucking good. Also, why was his tongue so warm? Weren't vampires cold-blooded? Ugh, everything about Ares was confusing.

The pain disappeared almost instantly with the swipe of his tongue, but even after he stopped, he was standing far too close for comfort. I did the grown-up thing and slipped under his arm so I could get some distance between us once again.

There was no part of me that wanted to go back into his arms—or at least that was the story I was sticking to at the moment.

I hadn't asked for this. What the fuck was I going to do?

"Okay, I allowed you to help me. You should start talking now," I said petulantly, not grateful at all since he was the one who'd made me bleed in the first place.

Ares turned and leaned against the wall, his eyes tracking my every movement. There was a shiver tingling along my skin as his gaze traced my skin, and I wrapped my arms around myself to try and ignore it.

"What do you want to know?" he asked in a gravelly voice. My eyes dipped down as if he was compelling me, and I saw a rather large tent in his pants. Evidently, the whole touching thing hadn't left him unaffected either.

"Who are you?" I asked, ripping my gaze back to his face.

"I'm the leader of the hunters," he said unflinchingly, his eyes locked on mine.

I stutter-stepped backwards, my mouth dropping open.

"What?" I gasped.

"I was adopted when I was a boy by a hunter who found me wandering alone. I learned quickly that the higher up I was in the organization, the more control I had and the closer I could get to my goals." His gaze flicked over me, reminding me that I happened to be one of his goals. Or maybe even his main goal. "I've been using those vampires down there to help with my hunt."

"So you're a wolf killer," I finally said when I'd recovered from the shock of his last statement.

He nodded slowly, his eyes still locked on mine.

"And you've been hunting me," I said in a whisper.

He nodded again and I began to get frustrated. It was like pulling teeth to get any answers out of him. I'd like a good long monologue about now. Isn't that what the villains always did in the movies? Spilled their guts right before they were going to end you.

"The least you can give me after everything you put me through today, is to tell me what you meant downstairs," I growled.

Ares had just opened his mouth when I heard a choir of raucous yells coming from down the hallway. There was screaming and chanting, and it slipped through the cracks of the door, accompanied by heavy footsteps coming closer.

"Fuck," he muttered. "That was quicker than I thought." In a flash, he was standing right in front of me. He grabbed my wrist and began to tug me towards the window. Ares shoved it open and then stuck his head out, looking left and right and down. "You're going to have to leave this way," he said, a thread of urgency in his voice.

The yells and chants were getting louder, and at that point, it sounded like a herd of elephants was right outside the door.

And then the banging started.

Terror threaded its way through my gut. I hated being this defenseless. My wolf shuddered in agreement inside of me, both of us desperate for her to come out. Banging started on the door, and a low growl ripped from Ares's chest.

I peeked out the window and bit my lip at how far of a drop it was. How exactly did he think I was going to be able to do that without my wolf? Maybe this was how I died.

Ares pulled keys from his pocket and stuffed them into mine. The door shook again, and I held in a cry when a fist emerged through the wood, the loud, desperate-sounding yells of the vampires filling the room.

"What's wrong with them?" I asked, my eyes flicking crazily from the outside drop he wanted me to take, to the splitting wood of the door.

"I was an idiot and didn't clean up the blood that dripped on the ground before we came up here. I was just trying to get you away from the situation. But by the sound of it, the whole group is under bloodlust." The hole got bigger, and another fist burst through to join the other. I felt like I'd found myself in a scene from that show, *The Walking Dead*, where the zombies were clawing their way into where the terrified people were hiding, desperate to taste flesh.

This was without a doubt one of the most terrifying moments of my life, but somehow with Ares standing here, it didn't seem quite as scary as it should have.

"Here, I want you to take this," he murmured, ripping a necklace I hadn't noticed from his neck. He moved to put it into my hand.

The moment the stone touched my skin...I was somewhere else.

"I'm going to find you," I heard Mother laugh as she got closer to where I was hiding behind an old cupboard in the kitchen. The kitchen staff was hustling around and shooting us amused glances as my mom pretended to look around. I knew that her wolf could smell me, but it was still so much fun to play hide and seek with her because she always acted like she couldn't find me.

She was just a few steps away when a horn blared out from the kitchen window. Mom froze, and I stuck my head curiously out from where I was hiding to see what was going on. She strode quickly towards the window, her posture tense. The acrid scent of fear ripped through the air, and I wrinkled my nose at the smell of the staff's emotions. What were they scared of?

Deciding I wanted to investigate myself, I crawled all the way out from my hiding place and stood up, dusting off my dress. That was maybe the only part of the castle that hadn't been cleaned, evidently.

"Mom? What's going on?" I asked curiously, watching her frozen form as she stared at something out the window. The sound of my voice seemed to break her from her trance and she whirled around towards me, a slight tremble to her lips.

"We have to go now," she barked, her wolf coming to the surface and hovering where I could see it in her eyes.

"All of you, slip out the back and run towards town," she ordered the trembling staff. They didn't hesitate to listen, scrambling over themselves to leave the room.

"Mommy, what's going on?" I asked her in a tear-filled voice. One thing about my life, it wasn't scary, and bad things didn't happen, so I didn't understand what was going on now.

"Come on, Rune. We have to go find your father. Now," she said as she grabbed my hand and pulled me towards the back hallway. We made it halfway down when she pulled us to a stop and pressed something in the wall. My mouth gaped open when

a large opening appeared as the stone wall pulled away. "This will take us straight to your father's office, darling," she whispered. I jumped when a scream tore through the air, sounding like it was coming from outside the kitchen—near where the staff had just left.

"Hurry, Rune." My mother pulled me up the set of narrow stone stairs, and I trembled as the stone wall slid closed behind us, blocking out the screams that had continued down the hall.

My wolf hadn't come out yet since I was so young, but I could feel her pacing anxiously inside of me like she wished she could. I slipped and almost fell down the stairs, and my mother caught me just in time. She didn't say anything, just continued to pull me behind her as we went round and round until the stairs abruptly ended in front of us. She pressed another stone in the blank wall in front of us, and the door slid open. My father's form filled the entryway.

"What are we going to do?" my mother gasped as my father pulled both of us into his arms.

"We'll get you both out of here," he promised, but my mother was already shaking her head against his chest.

"I'm not leaving you."

I whimpered and their gazes both dropped to me. My father pulled us further into his office which was in the East tower, as high up in the castle as you could get.

Somehow, even up here, I could still hear screams floating in from the window.

Mother darted towards Father's desk and picked up the phone there, pressing a button and lifting it to her ear.

"Please pick up. Please pick up," she chanted, visibly sighing in relief when a worried voice floated through the phone.

"You have to take Rune."

I was pulled from the scene with an audible gasp when Ares grabbed my arms and yanked me forward until I was plastered against him. He kissed me aggressively, his tongue slipping into my mouth with deep long strokes that lit up my insides and distracted me from the achingly familiar scene I'd just witnessed in my...vision?

It was ridiculous, but when he pulled away, a whimper slipped out of me and my body pressed closer to him. That smug, satisfied grin of his lit up his face once again.

"There will be more of that soon, sweetheart," he said, his words a promise. There was another crash as more of the wood splintered. His spell must've been a good one, because the locks were still holding firm. It was just the middle of the door that was being frantically torn away.

"Take my car, and that necklace, and get back to those assholes as fast as possible so they can take care of you until I can get back to you," he said calmly.

I heard chanting on the other side of the door, floating in through the hole in the middle. The locks began to glow like they had with Ares.

Ares rolled his eyes. "Of course, Cody decided to get involved," he muttered, shaking his head.

I ignored what he'd said about getting back to me and glanced at the broken blue stone hanging from the necklace. It definitely had magical powers, judging by what I'd just witnessed.

"What is this for?" I asked as he scooped me up and sat me down on the window ledge. My gaze darted down below. But just as I began to panic, his arm reached above us and pulled out a rusted iron ladder that he continued to pull until it was extended all the way to the ground. There was another crash at the door, and I jumped onto the ladder, hanging there as I locked eyes with Ares.

"That stone is what's going to help get rid of the spell the fae put on you. You just have to find the other half."

I began to descend again when the top lock broke off and the top of the door bent forward as if it was rubber and not wood. Goosebumps broke out over my skin.

"How do I find the other half?" I asked frantically as I made it down another step.

"The stone of Adelaide. I'm sure you can find information about it in that fancy library in town," he said. He seemed completely nonplussed about the crazed hunters... vampires—whatever they were—that were about to descend on him.

"What's going to happen to you?" I asked, annoyed at the worry leaking into my voice.

Whatever it was that had happened between us needed to go. Immediately.

"I'll be fine, Rune. Just stay safe until I can get to you, baby." I heard the door rip open and footsteps burst into the room. I hustled down the rest of the ladder until I was safe on the ground, sprinting to the left where I could make out the road. I was pretty sure that's where we had parked. I couldn't help but look back as I ran, locking eyes once more with Ares as someone leapt on him from behind. He held my eyes for far too long before turning and ripping the head right off of the vampire who'd just attacked him.

Maybe he'd be fine after all.

"You're mine, Rune," he growled after me, the sound of his voice echoing through the alleyway. As I made it to the corner and turned, I sighed in relief when I saw his car out front and no one around.

I was almost surprised when the car door unlocked, and I was able to get in, start it, and zip away.

My thoughts were racing as I tore down the road. What was that vision? And how the hell was I going to explain what had just happened to Wilder and Daxon?

2

The windshield wipers swished back and forth, rain splashing everywhere. It would have been hard to drive Ares' Chevy on a normal day, but with the fact that night had fallen, and it was pouring rain, the car seemed to have a mind of its own as it swerved all over the road.

My knuckles were white with how hard I gripped the steering wheel, though that might have had everything to do with what I'd just gone through.

For a long time, I'd believed I'd been cursed—bad luck followed me constantly. After moving to Amarok, I started to hope that I might have been wrong.

But deep in the pit of my gut, I was starting to doubt myself once more.

Because if my life wasn't complicated enough, I now had an obsessive vampire on my heels. I couldn't even give thought to the whole cryptic explanation Ares gave me...or that somehow we were a blood match—what he seemed to call fated mates.

That did my head in as much as it did to watch him

attack his own men to protect me as he let me go. Just like that.

How was I supposed to make sense of that?

The stone necklace he gave me sat heavily in my pocket as a reminder that I hadn't just dreamed everything or had some kind of mental break with that vision of my mother. The woman I didn't recognize or remember that I swore felt like my mother. Thinking back, there was a lot from my younger days that seemed unclear, and most of my memories were blurry.

The vision just added to my confusion over my past.

Did I mention that my life had become extremely complicated?

Darkness rose within me as my insides sank with the feeling that everything had become too much.

Sighing, I drove down the main road in town, the car's lights carving through the night. I'd messaged Daxon and Wilder, but no one had responded, and I kept getting no signal when I tried to call them.

I just wanted to get out of this freaking town.

The road was quiet with barely any cars, and I tried my best to remember the way back to Amarok. All of a sudden, up ahead, several men spilled onto the road in an explosive brawl.

My heart skipped a beat at the sight, and I slammed my foot on the brake pedal. The back tires fishtailed across the wet road.

Frantically, I tried to control the steering wheel, while my eyes bulged at the sight in front of me.

One of the men drove a boot into the other's chest, hurling him right across the road and tumbling into someone's front yard.

My chest thumped because of course, my initial thoughts flew to them being vampires. They'd found me!

The car came to a screeching halt, feet from the battle. I gasped for air at how close I'd come to running them all over. My car lights lit up the fight, when a heaving, huge beast of a man rose to his feet, twisting in my direction.

Bulging muscles, blood running down his cheek, he sucked in a deep breath. His shirt had been ripped, his jawline covered in a light stubble.

Piercing green eyes I recognized instantly clashed with mine. Black hair stuck to the sides of the most gorgeous face. I choked on my breath.

"Wilder," I squeaked.

His gaze was glued on the car, eyes squinting, trying to look past the lights in his face.

A muffled cry ripped from my throat, half desperation and half sob. Shoving the gear into park and pulling up the hand brake, I scrambled out of the car and into the rain.

"Wilder," I called to him, tears filling my eyes, and my chest close to breaking.

"Rune!" His gaze widened at seeing me, and then we were running towards one another.

In a flash, he whisked me into his arms, and my feet lifted off the ground. He peppered my face with kisses, and I wasn't sure if I was crying or laughing with such happiness that we'd found each other.

Everything between me and my men was complex, but at the same time, I knew they were mine. My heart thrummed with excitement, and he held me with such possessiveness, that it told me he'd never let me go again.

"Rune, I thought I lost you," he growled, barely able to string two words together. Then he kissed me, rough and primal, completely savage like he might fuck me right in the middle of the road. He tasted like rain and smelled of wolves and the woods. And god, he was my everything.

Someone suddenly tugged on my arm.

I twisted around with a gasp towards a strange man I'd never seen before who was throwing a punch right for my face.

I cried out as Wilder dropped me out of his arms, his hand flying at the man's fist.

Falling to my feet, I stumbled backward as Wilder turned feral. It was the best way to describe what I watched. He snatched the man's hand and snapped his wrist with one abrupt twist.

The man howled, and Wilder attacked, wolf teeth and claws extending. Glancing up through the rain, I saw that it was a full moon, meaning Wilder could shift. A pained moan brought my gaze back to the scene of the battle. Blood spurted in every direction. Wilder snarled ferociously, gripping the man by the throat. He ripped it out before the man hit the ground.

"That's for fucking daring to touch what's mine," he spit, throwing the bloodied throat onto the ground next to the dead man. Then he wiped his bloody hand on his pants.

I sucked in rushed breaths, my chest on fire with each inhale. Stars blinked behind my eyes at the shock of what I'd seen. Wilder had been hanging out with Daxon too long.

"You didn't need to kill him," I breathed.

He twisted in my direction, a haunting ache in his eyes. "If he's not breathing, he can't touch you. No one hurts you."

My body ached all over, and even though I had no clue who these strange men were, I trusted they were enemies.

He wiped the blood off his cheek with the sleeve of his shirt, striding back towards me. His gaze lingered over my body, studying me carefully as if searching for something, then paused on my neck.

"That fucker, Ares, bit you?" he snapped, reaching for my injured neck. It had stopped bleeding a while ago after Ares's...lick, but the mess remained on my skin. "Tell me he didn't drink your blood, Rune."

I bit my lip. Ares had definitely sunk his teeth into my neck, and it wouldn't be the first time he drank my blood either. But then he'd also stopped his vampires from attacking me. I was feeling very confused about him at the moment.

"It doesn't really hurt," I finally said. My hand went to my neck, the skin still tender from where Ares had fed on me.

"Oh, Rune." He drew me into his arms. "You're ruining me. Our world is full of monsters. They may look like angels, but beneath the masks they wear, they thrive on harming others like you."

My heart fluttered at the way he stared at me so lovingly, so painfully. He killed for me, and instead of terror, I loved every inch of him. People had hurt me my entire life, so to finally have two men who'd do anything to get revenge on my behalf...well, it was slightly exhilarating.

It was in that same moment when I noticed movement from behind Wilder.

Daxon was standing up.

My heart beat faster. I'd somehow missed him in the rain and dark, but now I saw that he'd been battling three men on his own.

The three dead men were slumped on the side of the road in a bloody heap.

"Fucking rogue wolves," he growled, but when his gaze

lifted and locked onto mine, his anger morphed into an expression of utter bliss, and I almost felt like he might cry.

I ran to him, needing to feel him, to know that I wasn't imagining any of this. Plus, I might have been crying too.

"Rune, sweetheart." His voice cracked as I threw myself into his arms. Our mouths clashed, and he kissed me like he was attempting to inhale me into him. "I was ready to torch down the whole fucking world to find you. But fuck, I'm going to destroy Ares for taking you," he breathed against my mouth. I had no doubt that Daxon would go ballistic on Ares when they crossed paths next. The vampire deserved it... and yet part of me wasn't ready for that either.

I was a complete mess.

He leaned closer and kissed me endlessly, his body wrapped around mine. "I missed you every second you were gone. You have no idea how frantic I became when I received your voicemail. I tried calling back, but there was no signal." He kept on kissing me like he was attempting to imprint the memory in his mind. "I'm nothing without you, Rune. Nothing. Please, babe, I can't lose you."

Holding onto him for dear life, I whispered, "I'm not going anywhere. But there's so much I need to tell you."

The harsh blare of a car horn had me flinching, and Daxon pressed me against him possessively. A car was racing down the road towards us. We were literally in the middle of the road making out.

Daxon hurried us off the road, and that was when I noticed Wilder had dragged the bodies away on the opposite side of the major road.

"Who were those guys?" I glanced at the dead.

"Asshole wolves from a local pack who got in our faces. But who gives a fuck about them. Baby girl, you're in my arms," Daxon murmured, as he continued to hold me against his body like he was afraid that I was going to disappear at any moment. "I'm so sorry I let that prick take you. I should have done a better job of getting rid of him, should have done so much fucking more." His large hand ran across my cheek, his thumb tracing across my lips, and his other hand pressed hard into my lower back. "But you're safe now."

His words ignited a fire in my chest, and I bit my lower lip, staring deep into those gorgeous, hazel eyes. "That means everything to me."

"When you look at me that way, I want to rip your clothes off and fuck you right here. To show the entire fucking world that you belong to me."

"Why does that sound so beautiful to me right now?" I asked, but I found myself looking up and down the road, peering into the shadows. Every small noise had me jumping.

Fragments of memories from the bar with Ares and his furious vampires slipped into my mind, along with the fact that we weren't that far away from that town still. An ache flared in my chest, and the hairs on my arms raised because I didn't feel safe. Was Ares watching us now? Were the other vamps?

"I want to get out of here, please." I grasped onto Daxon's shirt, just as Wilder joined us at the edge of the road. The cars swerved around Ares' black Chevy, the engine still running where I'd left it in the middle of the lane.

"Where the fuck is Ares, sweetheart?" Daxon snarled. "I'm going to destroy him for good this time."

Both men stared at me, their gazes promising destruction. They were out for blood, but I just wanted to get out of there.

"He's a vampire," I murmured, while Daxon held me tightly in his arms. "Ares is technically dead, but there's so much more you need to know. I think he wants to help me. I mean, he even gave me his car to head back home."

"A fucking bloodsucker?" Daxon seethed as though he didn't hear anything else I'd said beyond the word "vampire", his mouth twisting into a hateful frown. "That explains so much." He and Wilder exchanged a nod on something I clearly wasn't privy to.

"Even the dead can die," Daxon told me. "Now, where the hell is he?"

I gave them instructions to the bar. "Except I doubt he'll be there now. And I don't want to go back." With how many vamps there were and how they'd bent that door, I didn't want my men going there at that moment either.

Wilder reached over, his hand stroking across my back, closing in on my other side. "You're safe now."

I melted against him, loving how they pinned me between them. These two incredibly gorgeous alphas were two sides of the same coin. One psycho, and one dominant. So beautiful and yet cruel as demons to anyone who crossed them. I'd given my heart to them, and I wouldn't change a thing.

"You're trembling," Wilder muttered. "We need to get you back to Amarok." Wilder's gaze lifted to Daxon. "We'll come back and finish this."

Just then, a bolt of heavy lightning streaked the sky, the ground shuddering. The rain was picking up as the storm worsened.

I groaned, and before I could even move, Wilder snatched my hand and guided me down a side street to where I spotted his car. "Let's leave before we get struck by lightning." I stumbled alongside him, looking over my shoulder at Daxon who ran in the opposite direction.

"I'll meet you down the road, just before the overpass," he called out, as he hopped into the driver's seat of Ares' car.

"What's he doing?" I asked.

"Something stupid, I'm sure," Wilder griped as we rushed to his car.

3

RUNE

Wilder fired up his car and flipped on the heater, while I buckled myself in my seat. I kept looking over my shoulder until Daxon drove off down the road, wondering if he had plans to go find Ares first?

Wilder placed a hand on my thigh, distracting me, and when I looked at him, he had heartache in his eyes. "A part of me died when I saw your message that you'd left town with Ares. I couldn't believe he'd taken you from us. That can't happen again, Rune."

I held his gaze, his breaths quickening. Wilder was a thunderstorm when it came to his possessiveness, and lucky for him, I loved the rain.

"I'm just happy I found you both on my drive," I said. "The only reason I survived was because Ares spared my life from the other vampires who wanted to tear me apart."

Wilder leaned towards me, his hand sliding to the side of my jawline, holding me in place, his lips on mine, a passionate kiss filled with yearning...with love. He whispered, "A monster is still a fucking monster, Rune. Don't make excuses for him. You wouldn't have been in that position in the first place if he hadn't taken you there."

I had no words because he was right.

He guided a strand of hair out of my eyes, and I was still lost in his gaze, unable to believe I had stumbled upon them when I needed them most. "We'd better go catch up with Daxon before hell knows what he does," he murmured against my lips.

I nodded and slid my hand onto Wilder's thigh, wanting to feel him, to know he remained right by my side.

The sky kept brightening with lightning streaking the night sky, and the rain picked up even more. I stared out the window as the outside world passed by. Homes grew sparser, and I kept an eye out for the Impala with Daxon in it, frowning when I didn't see it anywhere.

"Did Ares hurt you anywhere else beyond the bite?" Wilder broke the silence in the car.

"No," I answered. "But he said a few things that made me wonder if he's telling the truth. He knows about my past."

"Vampires don't tell the truth," he griped. "They're vipers and nothing more. I'm furious with myself that I didn't pick up on him being a bloodsucker while he was in our town. Fuck, that pisses me off."

"He fooled all of us, but he knows things and he gave me—"

"What's that?" Wilder asked, cutting off my words.

I turned to follow his line of sight at the field ahead of us. I squinted for a better look. The closer we got, the more the flames that licked the stormy night came into view. "Something's on fire."

The blaze grew wicked and out of control, shooting off some serious sparks even in the storm.

It was only when I spotted Daxon standing by the side of the road that it clicked.

"He burned Ares' car," Wilder blurted, matching my exact thoughts.

I had no idea how to react, but I ended up laughing because it was nothing less than what I'd expect from Daxon at this point. With the way he stood there, sticking his thumb out by the side of the road, as if pretending to hitchhike, he had me giggling uncontrollably.

"We should definitely get out of here," Wilder stated, shaking his head. Then he drove right past Daxon and pulled over at least fifty feet from him.

I rolled my eyes at their alpha struggle. Daxon raced up behind us and leapt into the back of the car, heaving for breath. Daxon was a huge guy and took up more than half of the seat, and goddess, he was breathtaking. All rugged, strong jawline, eyes that screamed sex, and a body I longed to ride. These two alphas brought out my sex-starved appetite, and just staring at them teased my libido. My body ached as my gaze lingered over him.

"Dickhead," he snapped at Wilder, ripping me out of my fantasy. Then Daxon glanced at me, with stars in his eyes, and shuffled over behind my seat. "And you, my sweetheart, come over to me."

With a snap, he unbuckled my seatbelt, and then his arms snaked through the middle of the two front seats, and grabbed me.

I couldn't even tell you how he managed it, but the next thing I knew, I was being wriggled out of my seat and into the back. "Whoa." I giggled, doing my best not to bump into Wilder, though my knee did whack him in the ribs.

"Sorry," I called out, then flopped down, half on Daxon's lap, half on the seat.

"No fucking in the car," Wilder snarled. "I'm driving."

I huffed. "Where did that come from? We're not —Ahhh."

Daxon's hand dove right under my skirt so fast that I lost my ability to think. In one snap, he ripped off my underwear and dragged them off me. I was completely unprepared for that, gasping for air at how quickly he took control.

"Sorry, Rune, but I need to tongue fuck you. I can't stand it for a second longer. I can still smell Ares on you, and I am going to fuck all of that out of you. I'm going to fill that sweet cunt with my cum, then spread it all over your body to get rid of his stink."

The car suddenly swerved, and I clung to Daxon. "Like fuck you are," Wilder hissed through clenched teeth. "I'll run you over before you fuck her while I taxi you around."

"Keep your panties on, asshole," Daxon shot in response. "I'm not going to fuck her just yet, and that was your rule, right? No fucking. Now just get us home."

"You bastard," he growled.

Wilder kept looking back at me through the rearview mirror. "If you want to come back to the front, let me know."

"She's fine here," Daxon stated, his hand pressed between my squeezing thighs. I was a mess of nerves and arousal, torn to see the tug-of-war between the men. Just having Daxon's hands on me and his lips on my neck, my panties were drenched.

"Pay attention to the road. Wouldn't want you distracted, Wilder," Daxon drawled.

"Dickhead," Wilder growled back. It was strange that their bickering felt comforting, like I'd returned back home.

"I'm fine," I said to Wilder, offering him a smile.

His grin melted me to my core, and when I glanced over to Daxon, his smile grew dangerously dark.

"I burned Ares' car for you, gorgeous," he told me, his eyes glittering, and I lifted my gaze to the blazing wreck we'd left behind. It almost glowed in the rain. "I'm going to destroy every last damn thing the vampire owns."

"The flames are pretty," I said, realizing that the longer I'd stayed with Daxon and Wilder, the more I'd discovered my own growing penchant for their darkness. Enjoying a burning car, cheering them to torture our enemies. Some days I could hardly recognize myself.

Daxon managed to pull his hand free from between my clenched thighs and traced small circles across the top of my thighs, heading north.

"Now, let's see how fast I can make you cum." He lifted me, as much as the back of the car permitted, and proceeded to lay down on his back across the seat.

"What are you doing?" I asked, half smiling because I never knew what to expect with Daxon. I balanced on the edge of the seat, my knees bent tightly, while Wilder at the front kept groaning under his breath.

"Come and sit on my face," Daxon ordered, and my mouth fell open. Well, he definitely had himself in the right position. Lying on his back, head flat on the seat, and his bent legs leaning against the other door.

"Like fuck you are," Wilder roared.

"Don't be such an asshole," Daxon gripped. "How about I do you a deal? I eat Rune's sweet pussy until you find a motel. Then she's yours." His hands were on my breasts, pinching my nipples over the fabric of my dress. They puckered at his touch, tightening so hard they hurt deliciously. I moaned, leaning into his touch. How was this even fair?

Torn between what to do next without upsetting either

guy, I felt stuck in some kind of mindfuck moment, because in all honesty, I was feeling a bit desperate to sit on Daxon's face. But when I looked at Wilder through the rearview mirror, he was fuming, and it hurt me.

"Agree to the deal?" Daxon asked. "Or is this too much for you to handle? We've been working on sharing. Right, sweetheart?"

"That's true, but this is a bit unfair to Wilder," I murmured as Daxon tugged down on the strap over my shoulder, peeling the fabric down and freeing a breast.

My moan only curled Daxon's mouth into a devious grin. His hands lowered to my hips, fingers digging into me as he drew me to twist and face him.

"I love the dusty pink of your nipples." He wrenched his neck up and drew one into his mouth, sucking, licking.

I mewled, my fingers digging into the door to hold on, my eyes squeezing shut as he burned me up. I just wanted him to have his way with me and make me forget the crazy day I'd had.

Every inch of me weakened as he let go of my nipple and breathed words over the tender flesh. "I'm so hard just inhaling your scent."

A shiver of excitement raced up my spine at hearing him.

He guided me, and I straddled one leg over his far shoulder, feeling extremely exposed to have my pussy right over Daxon's face.

He slid the fabric of my dress upward, scrunching it up in his fist and tucking it under my thin belt. His eyes never left his perfect view where I offered him all of me. He breathed heavily, licking his lips.

"You're dripping wet. Fuck, I love you like this." His

fingertips ran along the smooth skin of my pussy, then he opened up my folds, his gaze smiling at the sight.

I loved how intimate this was, how focused he was just on me.

"Wilder," I moaned, meeting his tight gaze in the mirror. "Are you okay with this?"

He didn't respond but growled under his breath, then on his next sharp inhale, he slammed his foot on the gas, and we were racing down the road. I lurched sideways from the motion, but Daxon's powerful hands were on my hips, steadying me.

"Tick tock," he teased. "Race is on, my sweet. Now sit down."

I settled over his face, tenderly, already balancing on the seat, my hands grasping the handle at the top of the door for leverage.

He pulled me down, and his tongue flicked out, taking a long stroke across my soaking pussy.

I whimpered at this touch.

"Rune, babe, when I say sit on me, I want you to suffocate me."

"Fuck, Daxon," Wilder groaned.

"Shut the hell up, Wilder. Now, sweetheart, smother me with your delicious cunt."

"Are you sure?" I ask, shaking from how turned on and vulnerable I felt in that moment.

"If I can breathe, then you're not doing it right."

"I can't–"

"Sweetheart, now," he demanded, with such genuine sincerity and passion in his eyes, that I found myself relaxing a bit. "Give me those sweet, sexy sounds you make," he ordered, purring the words.

I lowered myself further, his mouth on me instantly,

his fingers digging into my hips where he held onto me. His mouth latched on, kissing me, loving me with such sweet passion, that I shuddered. His lips and tongue lapped at my offering, his attention quickening. The whole time, he had his eyes open, dark and lustful, watching me.

I quaked with need while he dipped his tongue into my opening, setting me off. His tongue was warm and soft, yet demanding. Relentlessly, he devoured my slick flesh, his attention turning to my clit.

Crying out, I started to rock my hips, grinding myself against his face.

He groaned louder, his fingers digging into my hips, as he ate me ferociously. I writhed, my fingers pressed to the window, my breath fogging the glass, and for a strange moment, my thoughts flew to the memorable, similar scene in Titanic when he claimed her in the car.

Sucking on my clit, he was having way too much fun, and the licking sounds he was making should have been illegal.

We were flying past the world outside, and all I could see was darkness. No lights or anything. I held on with each abrupt swerve Wilder took with the car, feeling like somehow I was about to come on a roller coaster. And yet, Daxon wasn't letting me go either.

I was soaked, my insides turning to liquid fire, and I arched, moaning at the intense euphoria flaring through me.

"Come for me, sweetheart," he muffled with a full mouth, then the tip of his tongue flicked over my clit in fast, small pulses.

His words and his tongue stroking me sent my body right over the edge. Every inch of me grew tighter, the pressure coiled within me, and the orgasm hit as I completely surrendered to the beautiful bliss pulsing in my body.

I cried out, thrashing from pure ecstasy.

Daxon was moaning his own approval, eating me like I was a peach, licking up every inch of my pussy. All while I melted from the earth-shattering orgasm he'd just given me.

And in that very moment, the door I had my hands pressed against pulled open from outside.

I screamed that time for a very different reason as I started to fall forward...right out of the car.

Strong arms from outside caught me under my arms and dragged me out of the now non-moving car.

It took me a few moments to get my head straight and realize Wilder had me in his hold, and the car was parked on the side of the road somewhere in the middle of absolutely nowhere. My head spun, while my pussy still tingled.

"I can't take it anymore," Wilder growled, hand on my back, the other tugging at his belt and unzipping his pants. "I'm going to die if I have to listen to you moaning a second longer and not claim you as mine. Your sweet scent is strangling me. I'm sorry, Rune, but I need to fuck you before I burst."

My head still spun from the orgasm, my body thrumming, but I held onto Wilder's strong arms because my legs felt like rubber. "I want you," I murmured, still so savagely turned on, that I craved his huge cock inside me.

"You fucking bastard," Daxon emerged out of the car, the lower half of his face glistening with my juices. The sheer thickness of the bulge in his pants looked painful. "I don't see a damned motel here." He marched toward us across the damp foliage.

Wilder was a beast, his face torn between ecstasy and

fury. In a flash, he threw his fist out, striking Daxon right in the face. "Fuck your motel, you bastard. I'm fucking her now."

He grabbed me gently up and off my feet. I rapidly snapped my legs around his hips, and his tender kiss found my lips. "Tell me you want this, gorgeous, because I'll die if I go another second without feeling your sweet pussy tightly around my cock."

"Wilder," I gasped, the tip of his dick sliding along my slick entrance. "Fuck me, please fuck me hard." I clung to his muscular shoulders.

Footfalls came up from behind me, and I twisted my head to Daxon. To my surprise, he didn't attack Wilder. Instead, he stood there, watching me, heaving for breath. His deep gaze penetrated right into my soul. His hunger was palpable, as was Wilder's, but as I held his gaze, he unfurled the fists at his side.

"Eyes on me," Wilder commanded, his large palms on my ass, squeezing as he pushed deeper into me.

I sucked in a sharp breath, his girth stretching me, the delicious ache so beautiful. His mouth fell onto my neck, where he licked me, his body feeling like fire against mine.

He took his time, pressing inside me, making sure he didn't hurt me. His muscles clenched beneath my touch, and I groaned at how incredible he felt.

That was when I sensed something fiery hot against my back—a scorching hot cock stiffening against the crack of my ass.

I might have yelped at the unexpected shock of Daxon behind me with his dick out.

Wilder growled, his teeth bared.

Daxon snarled just as loudly, and a sliver of panic

crawled through me that we were going to end up in a massive fight with me between them.

"Please don't fight," I said, breaking their glares. "Right now, I'm dying to be fucked. Please don't take that away from me. I want you both at the same time." Arousal pulsed in my veins, my urgent need thumping in my chest. They'd both fucked me in the ass before...but this was going to be a whole different thing.

I was suddenly desperate for it.

"Are you sure?" Wilder asked me.

I was nodding before he finished speaking. "We talked about sharing, and maybe this is a perfect step towards achieving some kind of harmony," I said, as if being double-teamed was usually useful in brokering peace.

Both men looked unconvinced, yet neither pulled away nor threw another punch, so I took that as a win. "Now, are we going to do this or are you just going to tease me?" I said. "I've got a huge cock buried inside me, and I'm barely holding it together."

To my surprise, Daxon broke first with a grin. "You heard her. I'm keen if you are."

Shifting against Wilder's cock had him groaning, his eyes fluttering with how turned on he was. "Anything for you, Rune," he half griped, half moaned.

"I want you on my own," Daxon added with a fiery voice. "But I also won't lose you."

When Wilder moved his arms to my hips, Daxon greedily gripped my ass and guided his huge cock to my back entrance. He slid his erection over my slickness. I was so wet already, that when he pushed into me slowly, there was almost no resistance.

How could there be when I still glowed with an orgasm and was ready for more. "More," I gasped.

Daxon's cock steadily pushed into me, stretching me as he went deeper, and I tensed, holding onto Wilder's arms because neither of my men were small. They were huge, and he took his time to make himself fit. "Hell, you're so tight," Daxon grizzled.

With them both buried in me to the hilt, I felt utterly full. So full I could barely think. I shivered with how much I trembled with need.

"You okay, baby?" Wilder asked.

"I'm more than okay," I whispered, trying to find my voice which only wanted to moan. "Please, can you both fuck me now? I want to feel both of you move."

And on cue, they both started drawing out of me, then pressing back in, taking small thrusts at first, each of us finding our rhythm with our movements. After all, I had two cocks dragging in and out of my insides. The quicker they picked up their smooth pace, the faster they reignited my desires.

"Fuck, I can feel you moving inside of her," Daxon moaned.

I cried out, sandwiched between two alphas, quivering as they plunged into me. "Oh, God. I never want this to end. Make it hurt, fill me."

Daxon's mouth was on my neck, licking me, then whispering, "I love feeling your ass squeezing my cock. You're going to milk me soon and I'm going to flood your hole with cum until it drips down your legs."

Wilder stole my response with an enthralling kiss, his tongue plunged into my mouth, and he kissed me like he owned me. In fact, both men fucked me that way too. He nibbled on my lips, while I floated on growing pleasure.

The intensity of their friction became too much for me to hold back any longer, and the moment I let myself go, a second orgasm rippled through me. A glorious, explosive sensation that set off my nerve endings.

My screams bled into the night, and the men hissed their own desires as I squeezed around their cocks with my orgasm, catapulting us all into a world of ecstasy.

"Rune," Wilder roared just as he burst inside me, Daxon following suit. He snarled like a beast behind me. The three of us held onto each other tight, our primal sounds morphing into the most beautiful song I'd ever heard.

They filled me with their cum, pulsing, heating me up, while I drew in rapid breaths, grinning crazily at how good they felt.

Once they all settled down around me, we stayed there for a few moments in blissful silence, and I wondered if this was what it could be like if the two of them finally decided to get along and share me. The sheer joy of being loved.

Exhausted, I lay against Wilder's chest just as Daxon pulled out of me, but instead of leaving us, he remained against my back, leaving a trail of kisses across my neck. "You are so beautiful," he whispered, and I twisted my head to face him. Then I looked at Wilder.

"Thank you. I loved having you both."

Rain dripped down our faces, and in all honesty, I'd barely noticed that we were fucking out in the rain. But now that we'd paused and the rain picked up, a coldness raced down my arms.

"Let's get you in the car, sweetheart," Wilder said, then kissed my brow and pulled out of me as well. I missed them terribly and wanted to be back between their bodies.

Once we were in the car, I sat with Daxon in the back, wrapped in his arms for warmth. Wilder fired up the engine and cranked up the heater.

"Are you warm enough?" he asked with concern in his eyes.

"Yeah. Thanks."

Daxon rubbed my arms. "I'll keep her warm."

It was a strange thing to not have them bickering for a change. It was exhilarating to have them both obsessed over me rather than trying to rip each other's heads off.

Once we took off down the road, exhaustion tumbled through me, but I also wanted to tell them about Ares. So I broke into an explanation of everything I went through from the moment I arrived at the bar, to my vision, and most importantly, the necklace. I pulled it out of my pocket by the chain, not ready to tempt fate and touch the stone, just in case it sent me off into another vision.

Daxon was fingering the stone, staring at it closely. "So Ares told you this thing will remove your fae curse, but first you needed to find the second piece?"

I nodded.

"Why the fuck didn't he go find it himself if the answer is in the library?" Wilder asked from the driver's seat.

Shrugging, I answered, "Maybe he tried and didn't have any luck? But there's so much more I don't understand, and I think this blue stone holds secrets about me. Things that I think have been hidden from me."

"I'm more concerned about that sonofabitch thinking you're his. Fuck that to high hell and back," Daxon snarled.

I settled closer against him and beneath his arm, the whole day drowning me. "I feel like I lost bits of my life, and maybe Ares will be able to help me remember them," I told him honestly.

My eyelids closed with how heavy they felt. Amazing sex always put me to sleep. And what just happened...that was beyond amazing.

Wilder said something, and Daxon responded, but my mind was already drifting away to make sense of their words. Instead, the thought that circled around in my mind was Ares' last words to me.

You're mine, Rune.

"I don't like leaving her," snapped Daxon grumpily from the seat next to me.

I growled in agreement. But it would take both of us to get rid of a group of hunters and vampires, and even with him, it would be a challenge. Rune wouldn't be safe until they were gone—we didn't have another option.

Rune was currently surrounded by all of our betas. That better be enough to hold off any danger until we could get back to her.

Daxon pulled out his phone, and I didn't need to ask who he was talking to. I'd had to practically rip him away from Rune for us to leave, even though he was the blood-thirsty one of the two of us and should have been itching to tear off some heads. The problem had been Ares' scent was still all over her, even after we'd both fucked her, and she blushed every time she'd mentioned his name. If the guy had been in the room, I would have been trying to kill him again, even if the first time didn't work...just from jealousy. Rune had been a bit vague about why Ares had let her go, and I didn't doubt that he'd done something to get in her head.

The question was, how were we going to get his death to stick this time?

"How do you kill someone that can survive a meat grinder and pigs?" I mused, glancing over to see Daxon holding up his phone and taking a picture of himself as he gave a smoldering smile at the camera.

"Are you sending her selfies?" I growled incredulously, punching him in the shoulder when he lifted up the front of his shirt and took another picture with his abs showing.

He smirked at me. "Can't have her forgetting me," he answered.

I frowned and turned my eyes back to the road, wondering if I should take some pictures of myself as well.

I shook my head, trying to get rid of the ridiculousness, but the overwhelming need to possess Rune, to mark her as mine forever...it was growing stronger every day. It was taking all of my self-control to rein myself in. It was like my wolf was determined to keep trying to mark her until she finally decided to let me in. I brushed an anxious hand through my hair, trying to shake off the unsettled feeling I had that something was going to happen.

I'd been having those feelings a lot since Rune came into town.

"When I get through tearing him apart, we can put his body parts in different sealed containers. That way he can't regenerate and we'll have time to do some research on how to kill them for good," Daxon belatedly answered at least three minutes later, finally setting down his phone and tapping his fingers rapidly against the armrest, clearly agitated.

"That sounds good," I answered, a little bit awed at how

easily Daxon came up with different ways to murder people. I'd grudgingly come to respect his talent quite a bit since it was devoted to keeping Rune safe at all times.

I peered through the windshield, trying to get my bearings.

I'd been out this way once before but never gotten as far as to get off on the exit where Rune said she'd been taken to the bar. As we began to get closer, my mind began to get fuzzy and clouded.

Where were we going again?

Just as I had that thought, my wolf growled loudly in my chest, shaking off the mist that had begun to descend on my thoughts.

I looked over at Daxon and saw he had one hand pressed to his chest and the other one rubbing his temple, like he was in pain.

"What's going on?" he seethed through gritted teeth.

The mist tried to push at the barriers of my mind, and every time it did, my wolf would do something to bring me back.

"Magic," I growled. I took in deep breaths as I tried to focus. This was obviously where we needed to go since it was being protected so desperately. As we drove through a patch of woods, there were several times that I actually started to turn the car around. My wolf or Daxon would bring me back and we'd start driving once again. Daxon wasn't being affected the same way that I was for some reason. He was in pain, rather than confused. Maybe it was because we were different kinds of wolves. Both of our experiences sucked.

We emerged out of the woods by some miracle, and as soon as we saw the town in front of us, it was like a bubble had popped, and suddenly, my mind was clear and Daxon didn't look like he was being bludgeoned to death anymore.

"Why do I have a feeling that Ares had something to do with whatever just happened?" he muttered menacingly, his claws lengthening and then retracting in anticipation of seeing him.

I didn't answer Daxon because I was too busy looking around. My wolf was standing at attention inside of me, clearly sensing some kind of danger. There was nothing out of the ordinary about the town—except that there wasn't anyone milling around the buildings or walking on the sidewalks. It was like a ghost town, a perfectly kept up ghost town.

We drove down the street and soon found what we were looking for. It was easy to spot the building where Ares had taken Rune; it really did look like a building from some old western movie. I noticed that the front door was cracked open as we slowly drove by, but like the rest of the town, I didn't see any sign that the building was inhabited. I parked a block away and then turned off the car.

"We probably should have some kind of plan," I mused, keeping my eye on the rearview mirror just in case anyone came out.

"Why do we need a plan? We already have one. We go there. We kill every one of the assholes that thought they could hurt our girl. And then we find and capture Ares so we can take him back to Amarok, and hack him into a million pieces," Daxon said calmly. "With the way I feel, hunters or not, they're all going to be fucked for trying to take Rune away from me."

Away from us, I corrected silently.

That sounded completely reasonable.

"Well then, let's go. And try not to die. Not sure Rune would approve of that," I drawled.

"Not even death could keep me from her," I thought I heard Daxon murmur.

Rather than go through the front door, we decided to try the back. If Ares was smart, then he would have surely known that we would be coming after him. But the prickly feeling I usually experienced when there were hidden eyes on me wasn't anywhere to be found. It really was like no one was here. Daxon let his claws emerge all the way, and I pulled out my gun as we peeked our heads around the corner to see if anyone was guarding the back door.

No one was there.

Walking slowly around the corner towards the back door, I kept my eyes on our surroundings, expecting someone to jump out at any time.

"Where the hell is everyone?" Daxon murmured, sounding confused.

Unlike the front door, the back door was closed. Closed but not locked. Daxon went first, turning the handle slowly and then inching the door open while we hid behind it. There were no shouts of alarm, and when we peeked our heads into the doorway, there was no one waiting for us.

Daxon and I looked at each other in confusion before continuing forward.

We walked down the empty corridor and then turned a corner and came to a screeching halt.

Blood.

It was everywhere. Coating the floor and the walls. It was even dripping from the ceiling. Bodies were strewn all over the room. Or maybe I should say body parts. It looked like at least a dozen men had been ripped apart by the number of arms and heads I was seeing.

What the fuck.

Daxon looked perfectly at home as he walked through the enormous room, examining the bodies curiously.

"I don't see Ares's body in here," I commented disappointedly.

"I don't either," Daxon answered, kicking someone's head out of his path.

"Would he have done this?" I wondered out loud.

Daxon had stopped a few feet in front of the stairs on the far side of the room, and I watched as he crouched down and touched something on the floor, bringing his hand up to his nose and breathing in.

"It's definitely the right place. Rune's blood is on the floor. This must've been where he fed off her," he said, rage threaded throughout his voice. Just thinking about someone tasting her blood made me sick. Well, someone else tasting her blood. I was so obsessed with that girl that I'd welcome any part of her all over me, including her blood.

"I'll check upstairs," Daxon murmured before striding up the staircase. I kept on examining the bodies, noting the pure chaos of their destruction. This hadn't been a methodical kill. This killing spree had been done in a frenzy.

"Wilder, get your ass up here," I heard Daxon yell from upstairs. I jogged up the stairs and then down the long hallway until I saw an open door and a blood trail extending out past the doorway. I gritted my teeth in anticipation of what I was going to see.

Just like downstairs, everything was covered in blood and gore. There was another ten bodies up here and they looked to be in even worse shape than the ones downstairs. Daxon wasn't paying attention to the death around him; he was focused on the writing on the wall that had been drawn in blood.

Blood match had been scrawled messily across the wallpaper, and right under that, it said the word *soon*.

"She mentioned that he helped her leave, and that he'd said she belonged to him. She didn't mention that detail," he growled softly, the malice in his voice so clear that I even felt the urge to shiver.

"He definitely thinks Rune is his blood match," I stated, trying to think about what I knew about that. It came to me then, something I learned from some random book. This asshole thought that Rune was his fated mate. That's basically what "blood match" meant.

Oh, hell no.

Daxon walked over to the window where I saw a few strands of what looked like Rune's hair stuck to the wooden frame of the window. This must've been where she'd escaped from. Daxon savagely kicked someone's arm away and roared angrily, the ferocity of the sound setting off a flock of birds that were on the roof of the building across from us.

"He's not going to take her," Daxon said through gritted teeth that had begun to lengthen and sharpen.

I was in total agreement. Rune was mine—ours...

Ares was going to die because there was no way that we were ever going to give her up. That *I* was ever going to give up Rune. I'd already felt what life was like without her, and I'd rather die.

My wolf growled in agreement inside of me. I watched as Daxon darted towards the wall and used his claws to slice it up until the macabre message was completely gone.

"Let's get back to her. I have a feeling we won't have to

go hunting for him. He'll be walking towards his death on his own," Daxon growled, striding from the room.

I followed behind, suddenly desperate to not have Rune out of my sight.

Fuck you, Ares.

5

RUNE

"Latte, no sugar please," I said, while my gaze lingered over the glass cabinet displaying an array of pastries on the counter of Mr. Jones' cafe. These desserts were my weakness because the moment I got a whiff of their sweetness, I had to eat one.

"The custard tart is heavenly and was freshly made," Mr. Jones murmured.

I lifted my gaze to the man who always calmed my pulse. His white hair was wild today, tufts of it sticking out all over, a pen tucked in behind an ear, while he poured frothed milk into a cup of espresso, creating a gorgeous maple leaf design in the foam.

He glanced up at me with those huge blue eyes, peering at me just over his silver-rimmed glasses, and smiled. "Take a seat, sweetie, and I'll bring you exactly what you need."

"You always know just the right thing to say," I teased and shuffled around to a free table near a half-open window. Townspeople filled the place, and no one really paid me attention when I looked at them, but nonetheless, I still felt them staring at me. Including the gang of Beta bodyguards following me everywhere at Wilder and Daxon's command.

After Ares kidnapped me, my men had freaked out, and if I thought they were super possessive before, well, they'd just gone into crazy mode. But I couldn't stay in Daxon's house for a second longer without getting major cabin fever. So, with my entourage of Betas who were outside, I came for a coffee and a treat.

I had no doubt I was what the town gossiped about most of the time, and yet despite that, Amarok had started feeling more like my home than anywhere else I'd lived. And slowly, I was receiving more smiles from locals than frowns.

With a small grin from a woman sitting two tables down from me, I repaid the gesture and slid into my seat.

It didn't take long for Mr. Jones to amble over with my coffee and a custard tart on a plate, covered in a dusting of sugar.

"Enjoy, and there's more where that came from," he said with a grin, and before I could respond, he moved to the next table with their order.

The wind stirred outside, and restlessness whipped in my gut, my mind whirring on Wilder and Daxon, and their mission to finish Ares. Of course, it left me worried because Ares was unlike anyone I'd met before, but if anyone could handle themselves, it was my two men.

Without waiting another moment, I dug into the custard tart with the fork, and it literally melted on my tongue. I moaned softly because it was still slightly warm and simply heavenly. I had no idea how Mr. Jones did it, but everything at this cafe was decadent.

For those few moments, I even forgot about the fact that I was still under the fae's spell, that my wolf remained stuck within me, or that my nose bled profusely if I tried to force my transformation. That was the true test of a great pastry—if it makes you forget all the crap in your life.

Finishing it off, I wiped up the last crumbs with my finger, then washed it down with a mouthful of creamy coffee.

Before I could even lift my head to gain Mr. Jones' attention for more, he stepped up to my table with another serving. "Seriously, you are incorrigible. I will never lose weight at this rate."

He barked a laugh, the black apron around his middle jiggling with the motion. "Don't you dare, or you'll fade to nothing." Instead of leaving, he took a seat across from me, pushing the plate in front of me. "I love seeing people enjoying my creations."

"Wait, you made the tart?" I had always assumed he got them from someone locally who baked them in their kitchen.

"I dabble in baking sometimes. While I order most of the pastries, the tarts are my specialty." Something in his eyes glinted with pride.

"Well, it is delicious."

"Don't let me stop you. Enjoy it." His eyes smiled, and there was something beautiful about just sitting with a friend and talking about the simple things in life, like sweet, flaky goodies.

"You should market these and sell them around the country. You'll become famous. That's how good they are." I cut a piece and popped it into my mouth.

Mr. Jones rolled his eyes sarcastically. "I have more than enough adventure in Amarok for my liking. There's always something new happening to keep us on our toes here."

Swallowing my mouthful, I half laughed. "Sometimes

all I can do is laugh to stop from crying at how terrible things have been getting. But on the bright side, I am here and safe, and I have Wilder and Daxon."

He draped his arms across his stomach. "Speaking of which, do you know when they're returning?" Leaning in closer, he looked around the room, then back at me. "There's a small matter of a wild creature lurking in the woods near the town that needs to be taken care of."

I lowered the fork back to the table, my smile fading, remembering all too well when I last found myself waking up in the middle of the night in the woods. And I wasn't alone either... I trembled with the memory of what I'd seen that night, the memory pouring over me like ice water.

A creature as dark as the night on all fours, snorting. Hot breath floated from the corners of its dog-like mouth. Except, this was no dog or wolf. How could it be when it reached at least seven-foot on all fours and had razor spikes running down its spine.

Red eyes narrowed on me.

Goddess, I was going to die.

The creature's nostrils flared as it stalked toward me.

Panicked, I dragged myself backward on my ass, my hand patting the ground for a weapon, anything to help me.

It drew in a sharp inhale, most likely taking in my scent... and the blood from my nose. I was so stupid... talk about serving myself up as a meal to a starved monster.

I scrambled to my feet, clutching in my hand a broken branch. The beast came closer, and the ground beneath me seemed to slip with how hard I shook. My fingers tightened around my weapon, and I knew this was my time to sink or swim.

Running wasn't an option. My wolf wouldn't come out, but at the heart, I was still a wolf. And I'd not die out here like this.

"Get away," I called out with a shaky voice, lifting my weapon.

Never show fear to a predator.

Never run.

Always appear bigger than you were.

I had no choice now but to survive.

Snapping out of my flashback, the hairs on my arms lifted, and I met Mr. Jones' concerned eyes. "Did you see him as well?" I asked.

He nodded. "Very briefly, and long enough to know it wasn't a normal wolf. Others in town have been reporting similar sightings."

My skin crawled. "What do you think it is?"

He shrugged. "These woods are vast and dense, and mostly private land from outsiders. But what lives deep in these mountains is anyone's guess. I've heard some harrowing stories growing up here, but I mostly thought they were to scare kids. Whatever it is, it could have been drawn to town by the smell of food."

"You think it's looking at us as food?" I almost gasped the words, and lowered my voice instantly.

His jaw tightened. "I hope not. But before we find out, our two alphas need to deal with the issue. We've had enough deaths and missing people in this town to last a lifetime."

I couldn't agree more.

That was when Mr. Jones spotted a couple entering his cafe, and he jolted to his feet. "Enjoy your custard tart, Rune. Duty calls me."

He took off and left me pondering with dread the fact that something dangerous was watching the town and its inhabitants. What exactly had I seen that night in the woods? If it hadn't been for Ares who'd found me in the woods, would I have become the monster's first victim?

I lost my appetite at the thought and instead wrapped my hands around my warm cup and sipped from the nutty coffee. Peering out through the window, I stared at the ocean of trees surrounding Amarok, the mountains in the distance covered in woodland. I had never been fearful of going into a forest, but after speaking with Mr. Jones, doubt crept into my mind.

I'd lost track of time in the cafe, though I was just happy to have some free time where things felt semi-normal.

Knowing the Betas guarding me were growing restless outside—seeing them pace and even duck their heads into the cafe every so often—left me slightly on edge.

I was about to get up from my seat when my phone pinged with a message. Grabbing it from my pocket, I frowned. I had a new voice message, but I hadn't even heard the phone ring.

The moment I saw the caller, my pulse raced and I frantically hit the call button.

"Pick up, please pick up." My heart had been broken since she'd left town, and I missed her terribly. What I wouldn't give to have her with me so I could be there for her during her mourning.

After three rings she answered. "Hi, this is Miyu."

"Miyu, it's me, Rune, where—"

"You know what to do at the beep." And the message ended.

Oh, crap. It was just her voicemail. And here I'd gotten excited. Flopping back into my seat, I tapped the voice message button and listened carefully.

"Hey Rune, I've been meaning to call you for days now."

She paused, her heavy breath sighing over the phone, causing my chest to tighten, while in the background, someone was talking. Where was she? "In the end, it was easier to leave a voice message. Please don't hate me for leaving. I thought it would help. I miss Rae terribly. I can't stop crying, and everything reminds me of him. Everything, and I don't even know how to begin to get over it." She sniffled, and my eyes pricked at hearing the agony in her voice. "Maybe I don't want to ever get over it. I don't know anything anymore. I've tried everything. Even a new job to distract myself. But nothing has worked, and I'm starting to think maybe I don't want to get over him. I can't imagine a life without him. So, this is my wonky way of saying I don't know if I'll be back in Amarok."

The phone message ended abruptly.

"No. Miyu," I whispered, a sense of dread knotting in my stomach.

I searched the phone for a second follow-up message, but nothing. So I hit play again, and listened to it over and over.

My heart clenched, and something inside me was breaking. Hearing the grief in her words cut me to shreds. She loved Rae with everything, and just thinking how it would feel to lose Daxon or Wilder had tears rolling down my cheeks. The pain Miyu must be going through left me shaking.

She was losing herself and would end up broken... depressed. What if she hurt herself? My stomach twisted on itself, and at first, my body didn't move, refusing to carry me out of here. I needed to find Miyu, to talk to her, to remind her she was still loved, and that she wasn't alone. I needed to be there for my friend. To do something to help her through this.

I remembered her sharing that her parents weren't

fated matches, and that her father had actually run away from her mother when he found his actual fated mate. So poor Miyu grew up detesting the notion of such a match, and it was another reason she loved Rae so deeply. He wasn't her true fated mate, and yet they'd found true love.

The kind of love that was once in a lifetime, when all the stars in the universe aligned. And she'd lost it.

A small, strained sound tore from the back of my throat, and I sat there for a silent moment, trying to coax the tears back, to stop myself from crying.

So instead, my mind went over everything Miyu had told me about her past... anything to let me work out where she could be.

That was when I remembered hearing something strange in the background of Miyu's voice message. I was certain I kept hearing someone saying the word *miracle*.

I listened to the voice message again and again, especially across the part where Miyu paused. It took several tries, but that was when I heard it.

Miracle Library.

I googled the name, and I found it instantly. There was only one library with that name in the entire country, and it was located in Las Vegas.

I literally leapt out of my seat. Sure, she asked for space but I knew deep down my friend needed me.

I had to call the guys, convince them of my plan, so I hit the first number on my phone, which happened to be Wilder, as I left the cafe, the Betas following me just as Wilder answered.

"Babe, what's going on?"

"Will you be back soon? I'm thinking Miyu needs us and we need to go find her."

6

"How far away is Las Vegas?" I asked, watching the waterfall descending majestically from the mountain just ahead of us.

"About six hours," Wilder answered.

"I would've thought that she would've gone farther away," Daxon commented from next to me, his fingertips softly rubbing the top of my hand and sending goosebumps up my arm.

Daxon and I were seated in the backseat while Wilder drove...again. Daxon had pitched a huge fit when Wilder had opened the passenger door and tried to get me inside. You would have thought it would have been Wilder's turn, but Daxon had argued that Wilder had interrupted him on our previous drive. They'd eventually ended up flipping a coin to see where I was sitting, and Daxon had won.

So here I was.

I personally didn't feel like it was possible for me to lose in this situation. The only thing better than being snuggled up to Daxon would be if the car was driving by itself and Wilder was on my other side.

It was still kind of strange to get used to the little moments of peace between Daxon and Wilder. They'd been so insistent that I was only going to belong to one of them, but after everything that had happened, things had changed. There was an easiness between them that had never been there before. While they bickered and got jealous, it wasn't nearly as big of a deal as it used to be when one of them would touch me around the other. There was still part of me that felt guilty that I'd somehow fallen in love with both of them. But the other part of me—the much bigger part—knew that it would be impossible to ever give one of them up. I'd already experienced what it was like to lose one of them when Wilder had walked away. If it happened again, I wasn't sure that I could ever recover.

Wilder had a country song playing on the radio, and a song came on that I actually recognized. I hummed along as I looked out the window. I hadn't gotten that much time to admire where exactly I'd ended up so many months ago. This part of the country was gorgeous in every way.

I was so focused on looking at the scenery, that it took me a second to realize that Daxon's hand had slipped from my hand to my leg, and he was softly trailing his fingers up and down the inside of my thigh. I shivered at the sensation and shot him a look, but his head was facing the window, like he had no idea that he was beginning to drive me crazy.

I jumped when his hand slipped up my shorts and got dangerously close to my panty line. My loud gasp caught Wilder's attention and his eyes met mine in the rear view mirror. "Everything okay, sweetheart?" he murmured.

I wasn't sure what I should do. If I should smack Daxon's hand away, or...rational thought left me when his fingers slipped under my panty line and started to softly stroke my skin, briefly brushing my clit before he resumed his maddeningly slow strokes, too far away from where I was suddenly desperate for him to touch.

"Rune?" Wilder asked again, and Daxon chuckled darkly next to me, finally turning towards me with a knowing smile on his face.

Wilder hit the steering wheel suddenly. "You've gotta be fucking kidding me, Daxon," he growled. "Don't pull this crap again. I can smell her arousal. You're going to make me drive this car off the road. I almost crashed last time."

"Then pay attention to the road," Daxon snapped smugly.

Daxon must have been waiting for Wilder to say something, because he was suddenly slipping his fingers under my underwear, and through my folds, before thrusting two fingers roughly inside of me. I found myself arching against the seat, my legs spread open as I panted desperately.

Wilder glanced backwards, his eyes widening as he groaned loudly.

"Fuck, you're going to kill me, baby. You look so fucking hot."

I couldn't talk as Daxon began to fuck me with his fingers. The best I could manage was a wanton moan. Daxon's eyes were glued to where his fingers were moving in and out of me. My eyes flicked up to meet Wilder's gaze, which was going back and forth between the road and the rear view mirror. He looked confused...and turned on. His cheeks were flushed and his pupils were blown out. He was definitely battling the fact that he was turned on watching another man pleasure me.

"You're so fucking hot, sweetheart," Daxon murmured as he briefly pulled out his fingers and began to tease me by running his fingers softly against my entrance. "I dream about this, seeing you cum, hearing your sweet little moans, smelling you...feeling you. It's fucking everything."

"Fuck, fuck, fuck," Wilder muttered as the car suddenly lurched forward and picked up speed.

Maybe I should have been worried about that, but it just felt too fucking good.

"Daxon," I breathed.

His finger slid down my folds until he was suddenly softly massaging my asshole. I froze and he leaned forward and slid the tip of his nose down my cheek. My head fell back and he suddenly bit my neck; not hard like when he was trying to claim me, teasingly like he was trying to distract me from the fact that he was applying more pressure with each slide of his finger.

"I'm never driving again. Ever," I faintly heard Wilder mutter to himself as the car lurched forward again.

I felt feverish and flushed. I bit my lip, and suddenly, Daxon's lips were on mine, licking and eating at them, swallowing my gasps as I came close to coming...just from his touch.

"Taste so good, sweetheart," he murmured against my lips, and I moaned, his words just driving me closer to the edge. Daxon abruptly pulled away from me and then used a claw to slice down the front of my shirt. He yanked down my bra and then his mouth was sucking at my sensitive peaks, scraping his lengthened teeth over the tips until I screamed and suddenly came ferociously.

"Fuck. You're beautiful," Daxon purred. I just whimpered in response as he moved his hands away from me. I was burning up. I'd just cum, but I needed more...

Daxon must have read my mind because he scooped me up and pulled me onto his lap. We were seated in the middle of the back seat now...so Wilder had a clear view of what we were doing. And he was definitely watching as much as possible while trying to keep the car on the road.

Daxon lifted me up with one arm and then slid my soaking wet panties down my butt and my legs before becoming impatient and just ripping them right up. While still holding me up with one arm, he reached under me and unzipped the front of his jeans before pulling them down a bit.

He wasn't wearing briefs. Because why would he? He'd obviously planned on this before we'd even left. Daxon began to slide his dick between my folds, teasing me. I reached down to grab his dick and get what I wanted, and he stilled.

"Behave, Rune," he said wickedly. My chest was heaving. I was so turned on.

Daxon finally took pity on me and grabbed both of my legs and pulled them open so that Wilder could see the beads of arousal on my aching core. Wilder slammed his head back against the headrest, muttering to himself. The car was basically driving itself at this point because Wilder's gaze was firmly locked on the image of me spread wide in the rearview mirror.

Daxon slid me up his body before slamming me down and impaling me on his huge cock. I screamed at the feeling of fullness.

"Fuck. You're so wet. So tight. So perfect. Sweetheart."

Wilder growled up front, taking my attention back to him. His hand dipped down to his lap, and the heat in my insides increased as I heard the sound of his belt opening and his zipper coming undone as he freed himself.

"This is so hot," I murmured, my eyes wide as I leaned forward to watch Wilder stroke himself with his hand while he watched avidly as I was stretched over Daxon's cock.

Daxon moaned needily as he began to lift me up and down his cock, the sound of our slapping skin filled the car.

I was lost. Pleasure was radiating up and down my synapses. This was so good. So fucking good.

"Touch yourself," Wilder abruptly ordered, his fist slowly dragging up his delicious dick. A car honked behind us and then passed us, but none of us seemed to care. I wasn't sure why Wilder was still driving. He should definitely come back here and participate, but something was very hot about him watching us like this.

It was something I'd always imagined, but thought would never happen.

I slid my finger to my clit obediently and softly circled it. Daxon thrust into me faster, and I gripped onto his strong forearm so he didn't buck me off.

"Just like that, Rune," Wilder purred. "Ride his cock. Use him."

"Holy fuck. That's hot," I said breathlessly. Making sure to keep my legs spread so Wilder had a good view, I tugged on Daxon's arms until he got the hint and placed his hands on my breasts. Then I took over, riding him in a slow rocking motion while his fingers pinched and pulled at my nipples. My head fell back against Daxon's chest...and evidently, Wilder didn't like that.

"Eyes on me," he snapped, before spitting on his hand and continuing to take care of himself.

"Fuck, baby. This is so good," said Daxon. I felt Daxon's breath on my neck and then he bit down. Warmth spread throughout my veins and I moaned.

"You better not mate her in this fucking car," Wilder growled, and the pressure of Daxon's bite lessened. I could feel his yearning to bite down harder, but instead, he began to nip at my skin, biting down hard enough that I'd carry his marks tonight, but not hard enough to break the skin and create a bond.

Although I was ready for that now, wasn't I? After everything the three of us had been through, my wolf and I were in agreement that we belonged to each other.

"I love when you bite," I breathed, and he moaned against my skin as I eagerly rode him. I lost myself in the moment. The car was full of the smell of our sex. Our three scents tangled together into an erotic perfume that I would have loved to carry with me everywhere. My arms went above my head and tangled in his hair as he continued to work my aching breasts.

"How is this so fucking hot?" moaned Wilder.

"Keep driving," taunted Daxon. "We have that reservation in just a few hours."

"Reservation?" I asked, not really aware of what I was saying.

"It's a surprise, baby," Daxon murmured. "Just like that. Keep squeezing my cock with that perfect pussy."

Right as he said that, he pinched my nipples—hard, and my orgasm burst out of me, so intense that I lost my breath and my head started to spin.

"You're so tight, I wonder if your pussy could take both of us," he purred, and I moaned at the mental image he was giving me of both of their cocks stretching me out. I met Wilder's reflection in the mirror; surprisingly, he didn't look turned off by the picture Daxon was painting.

Evidently, I was caught in a dream, because everything that they were giving me right now was more than I could have ever hoped for.

I was so wet that I could feel liquid coating the inside of

my thighs, and every time Daxon moved out of me, a loud squelching sound filled the cabin.

"Look down, sweetheart," Wilder purred. "Look at the way his cock is stretching your beautiful pussy."

When my orgasm hit I'd slowed down, and it had been all Daxon fucking me the last minute or so. At Wilder's words, his thrusts began to slow, like he'd decided to put on even more of a show for him.

Honestly, it was crazy that we hadn't wrecked the car yet, because Wilder had barely looked away from us.

My whole body was shaking, and it just got worse as Daxon's hand slid down the front of me until he'd found my clit. He began to rub it between two fingers, knowing just how to play my body perfectly. With his free hand, he shifted my hips so I was angled differently, and he was all of a sudden hitting another spot inside of me—a spot that made me scream with every pass of his dick.

"You going to give this to us for the rest of our lives?" Daxon asked roughly. I didn't answer. I couldn't answer. There was another orgasm building, and I'd apparently lost the ability to speak.

"Answer him," Wilder growled, his hand moving so fast up and down his dick it was making a slapping sound that echoed the sounds of Daxon moving in and out of me.

"Yes," I whined.

"Yes, what?" Wilder barked. Daxon was moving so slow in and out of me that I could feel every inch of him. They both needed to shut the fuck up.

No. I didn't mean that. Their dirty words were affecting my orgasms almost as much as Daxon's touch was.

"Yes, you can have me," I moaned obediently. "You can take me every day. Whenever you want."

Evidently, that was too much for Wilder, because he moaned loudly as he came all over his hand.

Daxon licked up the side of my neck and then began to fuck me almost violently. The changing tempo had me coming again, squeezing his cock so hard that he had no choice but to follow me into an orgasm.

"We're going to ruin you," he growled. "He's never going to have you."

I was so caught up in my orgasm that it took me a second to realize who he was talking about. And evidently, because of how turned on I still was, a picture of the two of them taking care of me along with Ares filled my head.

Fuck. Not thinking about that.

Daxon continued to fuck me slowly even after he'd cum, until I was practically crying from how sensitive my insides felt. Only then did he slip out, leaving me feeling empty with a hole I wanted to refill...immediately.

"Fucking hell," Wilder growled, and a giggle slipped out of me when I realized he was looking for a napkin to wipe down his hand. He looked back at me and growled. "Do you think this is funny? Just wait until tonight, princess. You're not going to be laughing then."

My insides heated up at his promise. What the freak were they doing to me?

Daxon had somehow found some napkins in the back, but instead of handing one to Wilder, he used them to clean me up. But I noticed that he didn't touch himself.

"You going to do something about that?" I asked, gesturing to his soaked dick.

"Why would I?" he said with a sexy wink that made my insides flutter. "I want everyone to know exactly what I've been doing tonight."

"Motherfucker," growled Wilder, bringing his window down and slamming his fist on the steering wheel.

Daxon slipped on his jeans and then wrapped an arm around me and pulled me back against him as he put his other arm behind his head. "Let's go, driver. I don't want to be late."

Wilder burst into a chorus of curses, while Daxon and I started laughing uncontrollably.

Who knew road trips could be so fun?

———

"We're almost there," Wilder announced, rousing me from the deep sleep I'd fallen into after my multitude of orgasms. I leaned forward eagerly, admiring the skyline of hotels and skyscrapers that lit up the night sky ahead of us.

I'd never been to Las Vegas before. I obviously hadn't seen much of anything after Alistair had gotten his claws into me, and I couldn't remember much traveling when I was younger. So this was amazing.

My eyes were the size of saucers as we sped down the highway and the lights of the Strip began to grow brighter.

"I hate this fucking city," Daxon growled as we passed a billboard advertising the upcoming *Magic Mike* show. Wilder snorted.

"Why are there so many billboards for lawyers?" I asked as we passed five in a row followed by one advertising a strip club.

"They don't call this place 'Sin City' for nothing," Daxon answered. We took an exit that brought us to the street behind the famous hotels that I recognized from movies. There was urgency to get to Miyu beating around inside of me. But the library was already closed at this hour, and we had no other clues to go off of. We'd have to try first thing in the morning when the library opened. I was just hoping that the library was the new job she'd mentioned in her voicemail. Otherwise there was no way we'd be able to find her in this huge city.

"Take her down the Strip," Daxon suggested. I could feel his eyes on me which was a heady feeling.

Somehow Daxon always made me feel like I was the most interesting thing no matter where we were or what we were doing.

I rolled down my window, and if I'd been in wolf form, my tongue would've been lolling out of my mouth like a dog as I watched the bright lights around me. We passed a replica of a pirate ship, and then there was a fire show at the next hotel. Flames fired twenty feet into the air to the beat of tribal drums as the people filling the sidewalk cheered and clapped in front of it.

"Wow," I breathed as we passed a hotel Wilder told me was called the Venetian. It was a perfect replica of images I'd seen of Italy, complete with gondolas going down a moat that led into the hotel.

And then we were passing the Bellagio, and I was watching a fountain show that had been set to a Lady Gaga song.

Farther down, a replica of the Eiffel Tower came into view, and I gasped in amazement as it began to glitter with a million sparkling lights.

I'm sure I looked like a little kid in a candy shop, my gaze bouncing all over the place.

"We'll take you to see the whole world, sweetheart," purred Daxon in my ear. I'm sure there were stars in my eyes as I tore my gaze from the view out the car and looked at the far better one hovering right behind me.

We passed three glittering hotels that looked like they belonged in Manhattan. Wilder pointed to the Waldorf-Astoria skyscraper where we were evidently staying. My eyes widened—that was expensive. Did we have that kind of money?

Before I could ask any questions, a replica of the New York skyline popped into view, and I craned my head, watching in amazement as a roller coaster soared along the top of the hotel. We were obviously on a mission here, but after we checked on Miyu, we could play just a little...right?

Past New York, New York was a medieval castle-looking hotel apparently called Excalibur, and then there was the familiar-looking pyramid shape of the Luxor Hotel. We drove a little further down and there was the famous Las Vegas sign. Wilder must have seen the yearning on my face, because he parked the car on the side of the road and we got out and snapped a few pictures in front of it.

After finishing, we returned to the car, and Wilder drove onto the street behind the hotels, driving until he got to the back entrance of the Waldorf.

I felt like a country bumpkin after we parked and walked into the lobby. Alistair had obviously been very wealthy, but he hadn't shared that wealth with me. I'm sure that most of the trips he'd gone on, he'd stayed in hotels like this, but he'd had his whores on those excursions, not me.

I waited for a second to see if I could feel anything after that thought—a pang, a longing... sadness. But there was nothing, not a twinge. Somehow my wolf and I had finally succeeded in becoming completely numb to the idea of him as our fated mate. A smile slipped on my lips, and all of a sudden, Wilder was there, brushing his mouth against mine.

"Love that smile, baby," he murmured, giving me a sexy wink that had my cheeks flushing because I'd just remembered his promise about tonight. He smiled at me knowingly. "You'd better get yourself ready."

Right after he said that, we got to the reservation desk, and he turned and started chatting with the hotel employee in a calm, even voice. Meanwhile, I'd turned into a puddle of lust again.

Bastard.

"Down girl. It's a good thing these humans can't smell like we can. If they were breathing in the scent of your arousal right now, I'd have to kill them all," Daxon murmured in my ear as he set his hands on my shoulders and softly squeezed. "And that probably wouldn't be the best way to start out the trip."

I rolled my eyes at his joke.

Or at least I thought he was joking.

There was a woman and a man helping Wilder check in, and they were staring at Wilder and Daxon worshipfully. It really wasn't fair for them to go out in public among mere mortals. The effect was too much.

Wilder finally got our keys, even though it was obvious that they were trying to keep us there so they could stare at my men. We walked across the marble lobby towards the sleek elevators, got inside, and started to go up. And then we kept going up, until the elevator finally opened and a uniformed employee was standing right outside. He gave us a small bow, like we'd all of a sudden turned into royalty on the trip up. I looked at Wilder and Daxon questioningly, but their gazes were suspiciously focused elsewhere.

We walked down the plush carpeted hallway until we got to a set of double doors about halfway down.

The employee, who I would soon find out was our

appointed "butler" for the trip, opened the doors with a flourish. My jaw dropped as I peered inside and saw the floor-to-ceiling windows showcasing the glittering city right ahead of us. There was a grand piano in the corner of the room along with several couches and white leather chairs. The front entryway was black and white tiled, but the large room ahead of us had a dark hardwood floor.

Now Daxon and Wilder were looking at me, identical grins on their faces.

The butler began to show us around the suite. There was a movie room, a gym, and a full kitchen with marble countertops and glossy black cabinets. There was a full dining room and a study. The bedroom was at least three times the size of the room I stayed in at the inn in Amarok. The bathroom was a black marble masterpiece with a steam shower and a Jacuzzi pool so big it could fit at least six people comfortably.

The butler kept going on and on, but I'd lost the ability to hear him. What the hell was going on?

When he'd finally left, I dragged my gaze away from staring open-mouthed at everything around me and gave a "what the fuck look" to the guys.

"What are we doing here?" I asked. "Did one of you sell a spare kidney I didn't know about?"

Daxon laughed. "We have plenty of money, sweetheart. We're from a long line of alphas. There just aren't that many places to spend it in Amarok."

Well then. Evidently, I had a lot to learn about my two men, because as at home as they looked in our small town, they looked equally at home amongst all the glam and glitter that surrounded us right now.

I was the one that looked like I didn't belong.

There was a knock on the main double doors, and a

second later, the butler had come back in, wheeling a cart with several dresses hung on it.

"As you requested," he said with a nod before quickly leaving the room.

"What's this?" I asked, walking slowly over to the dresses and tentatively stroking the silky fabrics. I looked back at them. Both of them wore gazes of satisfaction as they watched me stand there.

"I promise we'll do everything we can to help Miyu tomorrow, but we thought we could have one night of fun after everything that's happened the last couple of months," explained Wilder.

Excitement glittered in my veins.

"A night of fun?" Daxon drawled. "Was that not what we did in the car earlier?"

Wilder flashed his teeth and then socked Daxon in the arm so hard that if Daxon had been human, he would've flown across the room.

"Pick out a dress, sweetheart. And then let's give you the Vegas experience."

I felt giddy as I flashed him a smile and then turned towards the dresses. I was trying to choke down all the emotions I was feeling. This was almost too perfect. I was waiting for a bomb to go off or something, because even with my curse, Ares, and my worry about Miyu...this was a fairy tale moment.

And I hadn't had a lot of those.

7

RUNE

The dresses were all stunning, but there was a long one-shouldered black lace dress that caught my eye, and I immediately grabbed it and wandered to the bathroom to try it on. The nude material underneath made it look like I wasn't wearing anything, but in a sexy, elegant way. The dress went all the way to my ankles, but there was a long slit that went up the left side just a few inches below my panty line. My entire leg peeked through every time I took a step.

I'd never felt more beautiful than I did standing in the mirror in that dress.

There was a tray of cosmetics laid out by one of the mirrors in the bathroom, because of course a place like this would have something like that, and I carefully brushed gold eyeshadow on my lids and attempted to give myself a cat-eye liner.

That didn't look too bad.

After applying some red lipstick and putting a few curls in my hair, I was ready to go. I stepped out of the bathroom, and as soon as I saw Wilder and Daxon standing there in suits, I about passed out with how good they looked. Wilder was dressed in a classic black suit with a black dress shirt underneath, unbuttoned enough to hint at the perfect chest he had under it. Daxon was dressed in a grey suit that had a slight sheen to it, a look that only he or Wilder...or a supermodel could pull off.

"Wow," I breathed as I tried to imprint their images in my mind.

"Wow is right, princess," Wilder said roughly, biting his bottom lip as his gaze slowly dragged from my head to my toes and then back up again. Daxon looked a little starstruck, just staring at me with his mouth gaping open. I blushed, almost feeling like we were on a first date again.

In that moment it was easy to pretend like our problems didn't exist. Evidently, we were living out a fantasy life tonight, and I was more than okay with that.

Wilder and Daxon both held out their arms for me and then led me to the doorway like I was a queen. We took the elevators back down to the lobby, and I flushed as other guests stared at us as we walked by them towards the entrance.

There was a stretch limo waiting outside, and a half-hysterical giggle slipped out of me when Wilder and Daxon led me over to it where a man in a pressed suit was waiting. The man opened the limo door with a smile and we got in.

"Someone pinch me," I murmured as I looked around the luxurious interior. "Did the vampires actually suck out all my blood and I've found myself in the afterlife?" I joked, jumping a bit when twin growls came from both of them.

"Don't ever joke about that again," ordered Daxon, his hand suddenly on my throat and slightly squeezing. "I'd never let you get that far away from me."

My eyes widened at the fierceness in both of their gazes,

and I nodded. Daxon's hand slipped off my throat. His lips were suddenly pressed on mine fiercely, and when he pulled away, some of my red lipstick was smeared across his mouth.

Alright then, I'd put "the afterlife" squarely in the "do not talk about" column.

"Champagne?" Wilder asked, breaking up the intensity of the moment as he pulled a bottle out from an ice bucket beside him.

"Excellent," Daxon said. Wilder poured us three glasses, and I tried to wipe the lipstick off Daxon's mouth, but he caught my wrist in his hand.

"Leave it," he murmured. "I want everyone to know exactly what I've been doing tonight." The words were an echo of what he'd said earlier when I asked him about cleaning...something else up.

I flushed just thinking about him wearing me all over himself, and he smirked like the asshole he was.

We sipped at our drinks, none of us talking as we gazed at the city around us, so different from where we spent most of our time. We were going back down the Strip and then we got on the highway. I looked at the guys questioningly, but Wilder just winked at me, obviously intent on tonight's events being a surprise.

We arrived at what looked like an airport five minutes later. The limo turned right onto the asphalt near a runway and then stopped.

The door opened a second later, and Wilder smoothly slid out. I moved to follow him, but before I could step out of the limo, Wilder grabbed me and scooped me into his arms. Up ahead there was a helicopter, and I looked at him excitedly.

"Are we going on that?"

"You've seen the city from the ground, so we thought you should see it from the air as well."

I couldn't hold in my squeal as we got into the helicopter and the pilot handed us headsets to put on. Daxon and Wilder both checked my seatbelt harness a couple of times, Daxon especially seeming to like the sight of me being all strapped in.

Which didn't surprise me.

A few minutes later, with the roar of the helicopter around us, we lifted off the ground and headed towards the Strip. It took me a moment to realize that I had both Daxon and Wilder's hands in mine, in an iron grip. Evidently, I was more afraid of heights than I thought.

My fear slipped away as we got near the Strip though, and I could take in everything below. It was different up here; seeing everything laid out below was even more magnificent than it had been on the ground. The pilot began to sputter off random facts about the city, and I listened eagerly as we went up and down the Strip a few times before heading back to the airport. After landing, we thanked the pilot and got back in the limo.

"That was incredible," I gushed as I leapt towards Wilder and grabbed his chin before pressing my lips against his. I'd intended it to be a short, quick kiss, but his hand was soon wrapped in my hair and he was keeping my mouth against his hungrily as he kissed and licked at my mouth.

Before we could get too out of control, Daxon ripped me away from Wilder and onto his lap where I could feel his obvious erection under my ass.

Wilder growled and Daxon just clicked his tongue. "I have to protect the lady's virtue or we'll never get through the night," he said in a terrible British accent.

I was pretty sure this was Daxon's favorite new game, trying to see how sexually frustrated he could make Wilder.

It was pretty fun, especially because I knew that Wilder would eventually blow and I'd be the one benefiting.

My stomach chose that moment to growl...loudly. Both of them laughed, dispelling the sex hormones that had been flooding the limo.

"We'll be taking care of that next," purred Daxon as he wrapped his arms around me and laid his cheek on my shoulder.

It took us about fifteen minutes to get to our next destination even though it was really close to the airport. There was always nonstop traffic on the Strip. We were at the Wynn Hotel for dinner, and I grinned when I saw that we were eating at a steakhouse. As the hostess led us through the restaurant, my grin widened when I realized we were being taken to a table right next to a small lake. This place was crazy. It had everything.

"I'm starving," growled Wilder after we sat down and began to study the menu, looking a bit...wolfish. I blinked, realizing that we'd been winding him up this whole time in the three days he was able to shift, and his wolf was even closer to the surface than usual. It was actually shocking that we'd made it to Vegas with what Daxon had done to me in the car.

We placed our orders, and right after the waiter left the table, bright lights started to flash on the lake, and a show started to play on the waterfall on the other side.

"What's this?" I asked delightedly. Daxon leaned back and grimaced as a bunch of animated frogs started jumping around across the lake.

"It's called the Lake of Dreams show," he muttered. "And this was not my idea."

I glanced at Wilder. "I love it," I told him, turning my attention back to the show where three giant toucans with neon coloring were now entertaining us. Our food started to arrive just as the show was ending, and we all dug in eagerly.

Wilder had ordered three porterhouse steaks, and I swore that the staff were making excuses to fill our water and wine glasses every fifty-seven seconds just so they could see him put them down.

When we were done, I was feeling delightfully full. That had been the best dinner I'd ever eaten.

After dinner, we walked out of the steakhouse, and Wilder and Daxon both held my hands as we entered the casino. I could feel eyes on us, maybe because of how edible my men looked, or maybe because I was holding both of their hands, but I didn't care. In that moment, I was just so fucking happy.

I picked out a few slot machines to try and lost terribly before Daxon and Wilder led me over to a blackjack table and began to teach me how to play. And by teach me how to play, I meant watched as both of them took turns winning until the dealer's face was getting red. After a crowd had begun to gather around us when the guys had won twenty straight games, we gathered their chips and walked over to cash them out.

"Did you really just win $50,000," I whispered, feeling bug-eyed with how wide my gaze was at what I'd just witnessed.

"I'm almost offended at how surprised you sound," Daxon teased, sliding his tongue in between my open lips and giving me an indecent lick before pulling away. "What do you think we do during the long winter nights? I'll have you know that gambling's among my top three talents."

Wilder coughed out a laugh as he took care of exchanging the chips.

"What are the other two talents?" I asked.

"Fucking and killing, of course," he answered.

Well then.

After collecting their winnings, I thought that we'd return to the suite, but evidently, they had other plans because we were back in the limo, and then five minutes later we were in a crowded club. There were half nude women and men dangling from red fabric that was wrapped around their bodies as they performed aerial dances above the writhing crowd. Red lights flickered all over the dark room, and a thumping bass was so loud and insistent that my heartbeat seemed to echo the sound.

We went over to the bar, and even though there were people four deep, Daxon immediately got our drinks. The guys had reserved a table right near the dance floor, and Daxon slid into the booth with his drink. I moved to follow him, but Wilder caught my hand.

"Dance with me," he ordered gruffly, and I immediately followed him to the crowded dance floor.

He didn't take me far though; he kept us in plain view of Daxon who'd settled into the booth, his arms spread out next to him, and his gaze locked on mine.

Nervous energy started to buzz through my veins.

"Relax, sweetheart," Wilder murmured as his hips began to move behind me. "Move with me. Let's torture him like he's been torturing me."

One of Wilder's hands moved to my hip, but the other one moved up my chest, between my breasts, and up my collarbone until his fingertips were dancing across my neck as he pulled me against him.

Our bodies were molded together. His breath was warm

against my neck as his lips began to dance from my shoulder up to my neck.

"You're like a dream," he whispered roughly, and I shivered, my panties already completely ruined from the experience. Daxon's hungry gaze was twin flames staring at me through the darkness. Despite all the people around us, it was like the three of us were in our own little bubble.

I finally relaxed then as Wilder's hand on my hip began to guide my movements. All I had to do was follow his lead. The music swirled around us, vibrating through my insides. He was hard behind me, and I made sure to roll my body against his, again and again until he was groaning in my ear.

His hand slid down my neck, down my chest, until he was practically on my core. He pressed his hand right above it.

"All I can think about is being inside of you," he growled.

I moaned in response as his hips rocked against mine. Wilder's hand moved to where my dress was slit, and his fingers slipped onto my inner thigh.

"Do you want me to finger fuck you right here, princess?" he purred. "Do you want to cum around all of these people while Daxon eye fucks you right there?"

"Wilder," I gasped as his fingers danced near my panty line.

"Wilder, what?" he asked mockingly, his fingers swiping across my aching core over my thin underwear. "You want to be our dirty girl, don't you? You want to fulfill all of our fantasies. You want us to spread you out on that table and fuck you from every hole so that everyone in this club knows who you belong to."

Holy hell. Where had this come from?

I was here for it.

"More," I moaned.

"If you made me cum right now, would you get on your knees right here and clean my dick with your hot little mouth?"

"Fuck," I gasped.

Wilder's hand pressed against my pussy, rubbing my clit hard through my underwear. Daxon's eyes were glittering across from us, his gaze locked on where Wilder's hand was hidden under my dress.

"You're such a good girl. Aren't you, baby? You're always going to be our good girl."

A sudden orgasm ripped through my body, catching both of us off guard.

"Oh fuck. You just came," Wilder murmured delightedly.

I flushed in embarrassment, so turned on, it was ridiculous. I was actually tempted to just strip down and let him take me right there.

I was kidding.

Kind of.

"I think it's time to take this party back to the hotel, don't you think?" Wilder asked, and I nodded eagerly as he pulled his hand out from underneath my dress, grabbed my hand, and stalked towards Daxon.

"Time to go?" Daxon grinned, his face flushed with arousal.

"Yep," Wilder growled.

And back to the hotel we went.

And I didn't get sleep for a long, long time…

8

I woke up on top of a hard chest, strong arms wrapped around me. I sighed and snuggled deeper as sleep tried to take me again.

A muffled grunt sounded nearby, and my eyes flew open.

What was that?

I wiggled around and realized that I'd fallen asleep on Wilder's chest.

"Hi beautiful," he said softly. I blushed just looking at him as I remembered all the ways he'd taken me last night. He and...I looked around the room for Daxon and yelped when I saw him in a chair on the other side of the room, tied up with a metal chain that had been wrapped around him several times...and a gag across his mouth.

"Daxon," I yelled, trying to spring off the bed. Wilder caught me around the waist before I could go anywhere.

"I was just giving him a little taste of his own medicine, sweetheart," Wilder purred, sounding very proud of himself.

Daxon was staring at Wilder with murder in his gaze.

I couldn't help it. I started laughing...uncontrollably. So hard that my stomach hurt and tears were falling from my eyes. "Where did you get metal chains? And how did you even tie him up?" I gasped.

"I keep them in my trunk just in case," Wilder said nonchalantly, stretching his arms above his head and showcasing his mouth watering abs. "You never know when you might need them."

"You did this when he was sleeping?" I asked, wondering how I didn't wake up for that. I had been very tired after all the sex though.

"Yep," Wilder said proudly.

Daxon yelled something under his gag and another laugh escaped my lips.

"I'm letting him out."

Wilder reluctantly let me go, and I slipped off the bed and walked over to Daxon who was now giving me puppy dog eyes.

"You guys are ridiculous," I murmured, examining the heavy chains. There was a padlock on the back, and I held out my hand for Wilder to give me a key. He handed it to me with a smirk and walked into the bathroom while I undid the lock and started undoing the chains.

"Maybe he should keep the gag on. It was much better that way," Wilder called from the bathroom. I ignored him and carefully undid the gag and took it off Daxon's face.

"I'm going to kill that mother—" Daxon began, shaking off the chains. I cringed when they clattered to the floor loudly.

"The library opens in thirty minutes. You can do whatever you want after that, but let's get over there first," I said, wrapping my arms around Daxon's waist so he couldn't go anywhere. He immediately relaxed in my arms.

"Of course, baby."

Wilder chose that moment to come out of the bathroom wearing nothing but a towel, tendrils of water beading down his chest. He leaned against the doorway with a big asshole grin all over his too handsome face. "Well, that was weird."

Daxon made to move and I held him tight. "We're going to see Miyu," I reminded him, and he stilled again.

"Just wait," he said through gritted teeth, but looking up at his face, I could see the smile he was trying to hold back.

We got ready and walked out of the suite. I cast one longing glance behind me, thinking that our night had passed way too fast.

"We'll come back, baby," Daxon said, kissing me on the top of the head as he passed by me. I nodded and followed behind him, turning my mind to the task at hand.

It was time to see Miyu.

———

The library she worked at looked like a huge metal box from the outside. It was at least five stories tall and must have been constructed recently based on how modern everything looked. I much preferred Amarok's library which actually had character.

My stomach was tingling as we walked through the front doors and entered the cool, quiet inside. People milled about the stacks. There were rows of computers set up, and almost every one of the stations was filled up. There was a large desk on the right side of the room, and helping someone check out books behind the desk...was Miyu.

Her hair had changed. It wasn't a glossy red anymore;

she'd dyed it a dark brown, and she was wearing it in a severe bun. Her cheeks were gaunt-looking and it was obvious she'd lost at least ten pounds or more. It was her eyes that got me, though. Even from here, I could see how haunted they were. My heart panged once again at what had happened to my best friend.

"What if she doesn't want us here?" I whispered, panicking for some reason. I'd had this bright idea that I could try and channel some happiness into her. But now that I was standing here, I was freaking out that it wouldn't work. I hadn't used it since the fae queen had placed that spell on me. What if it didn't work?

"It's okay, baby. You can do this," Wilder murmured soothingly. I took a deep breath and began to stride across the room, my gaze locked on Miyu. I'd made it halfway there before she noticed me. Her face lit up when our eyes met, and then I watched as her smile slipped and devastation crashed across her features. The books she was checking out tumbled to the counter, echoing loudly across the silent room and garnering stares.

"Sorry," she said hastily, gathering up the books and hurriedly checking them out and handing them back to the person she'd been helping. There was another woman working behind the desk, and Miyu muttered something to her before moving away from the desk and walking towards us.

"Follow me," she muttered softly, grabbing my hand and leading us behind a row of books where there was a row of meeting rooms. She led us inside one, and as soon as the second the door was closed behind us, she threw her arms around me, sobs wracking through her body.

After a few minutes, she lifted her head and looked at me with a red-rimmed gaze. "I'm so glad to see you."

"I've been worried about you," I said softly, squeezing her again in a tight hug. "So worried. You sounded so sad in that voicemail you left me. We just had to come. I know you said you needed space..."

"This feels a lot better than space," she murmured.

Daxon and Wilder were leaning against the wall, watching us silently.

"Want to sit down?" she asked, pointing to the table and the set of chairs in the room.

I nodded and we all sat down.

"I feel pretty special that both of the alphas of Amarok came to see me," she tried to joke, but it just came out sounding hollow. Like all the life had been sucked out of her and she was just going through the motions.

"I wanted to try something that might help you. I didn't try it before because I'm not sure if I can even do it on command...but I would like to try now if you'd let me."

She looked at me questioningly.

"Sometimes I can...influence people's emotions," I said, launching into an explanation of the times it had happened and how it had worked.

"That sounds a bit crazy," Miyu said slowly after I'd finished, but there was a thread of hope laced in her words.

"I've had some trouble with my wolf recently, so I'm not even sure it's possible. But—"

"Please try," she suddenly begged desperately. "I'll try anything not to feel like this anymore."

I took a deep breath and smiled, trying to look confident even though I was going to be devastated if this didn't work.

"Okay, what do we do?" she asked, leaning towards me.

"Umm..." I glanced at Wilder and Daxon, and they both nodded at me reassuringly.

"I don't think I actually need to touch you, but maybe I will just in case," I said as I reached out and placed my hand on hers.

I tried to picture how I'd done it before. Those times had been accidents, obviously, but it seemed like during those times I'd been either thinking hard about the emotion or desperately wishing that the other person could experience that emotion. Maybe I'd try both.

It was actually easy to come up with something happy, a fact that caught me off guard just because for so long, happiness had been an impossibility. Since escaping from Alistair and coming to Amarok, there had been tons of pain, but the happiness...the happiness was unmatched.

Now to pick the memory that would do the most good.

Immediately, that night with my wolf came to mind. I pictured meeting her for the first time, the feel of the shift, the ground beneath my feet as I ran across the cold, damp ground. The perfect taste of freedom I'd experienced. I channeled all of that into Miyu.

After a long minute, I moved my hand. "How do you feel?" I asked nervously.

She gave me a halfhearted smile. "I don't feel any different," she said, obviously trying hard to keep the disappointment out of her voice.

I frowned, doubt freezing my insides. Maybe I couldn't do it. Maybe that part of me was gone, just like my ability to shift.

"You can do this, baby," Daxon said confidently, and maybe he had this special power too, because his confidence was enough to push me to try again.

"Let me try it a different way," I told Miyu determinedly. I put my hand back on hers and took a deep breath. I thought over and over again how I wanted Miyu to feel. Of how I wanted her to experience happiness again. Of how I wanted the ache inside of her to go away enough that she could breathe.

I wanted her to believe in the possibility of joy again.

I put every good thing I could think of into my thoughts, continuously pushing them towards her like there was a connection between my brain and hers. After a couple of minutes of trying, I was about to give up when, all of a sudden, a giggle slipped from Miyu.

She was smiling. Not nearly as bright as she once had, but the pain in her eyes was fading, and even her complexion looked brighter. It was working!

I didn't let go of her hand for another minute, continuing to pour all of my well wishes for her into our connection. Finally, I pulled away. Tears were gleaming in her eyes, but I could tell they were happy tears.

"I feel so much lighter," she said in a choked voice. "I don't feel like I'm drowning—like I don't want to exist. I can feel the pain, and I can feel how much I miss him...but it's not the only thing I can feel anymore." She wiped at her eyes with a trembling hand. "I can't believe you can do this."

I glanced over at Wilder and Daxon. Their eyes were glued to my face, pride etched into their expressions. I blushed under their attention.

Miyu snorted, her gaze pinging back and forth between the three of us. "Looks like things have improved between the three of you?" she asked. My blush deepened, just thinking about everything that had happened the last couple of days.

I'd definitely call the last couple of days with them an improvement...

"You could say that," I finally murmured, the deep blush in my cheeks telling Miyu far more than I'd wanted to.

She sat back in her chair, shaking her head. "Rune, I've never heard of anyone who can do this sort of thing. I mean, this type of magic...it's incredible."

"I'm just glad it worked. Without being able to shift, I was worried that I wouldn't be able to do that either."

I launched into an explanation of everything that had happened since she'd left. Ares, of course, was the shining star of the conversation.

She blinked rapidly when I finished. "Wow, girl. You've been busy." She cocked her head and bit her bottom lip. "What does the necklace he gave you look like?"

I'd given it to Wilder to hold. I was still very much freaked out by the vision that I'd had and was afraid to touch it and trigger something else. Wilder pulled it out of his pocket. He'd wrapped it in a white handkerchief when I'd first given it to him, and he unfolded it and laid it on the table.

She studied it for a moment. "I've seen that somewhere," she said, her nose scrunching up as she examined it. "You said Ares was a vampire?"

Daxon growled, obviously not excited about the fact we were talking about Ares so much right now.

"He's a hunter. So I guess he's a vampire, but he could be a hybrid as well," I answered.

I jumped when Miyu suddenly slammed her hand on the table and jumped out of her seat. "I know where I've seen that necklace before." She practically ran towards the door. "I'll be right back. I just need to grab the book."

She left the room with a pep in her step that hadn't been there before.

"You did good, baby," Wilder purred as soon as she'd disappeared from sight.

"I'm over the moon I was able to do it. But now I kind of feel like an idiot for not trying it before," I confessed.

"I doubt she would've even let you help her before. She needed some space."

A couple seconds later, Miyu was back, holding a book so old it looked like it belonged in a glass case in a museum.

"I was organizing books the other day, and for some reason, this was in the erotica section of the stacks," she said as she sat down and carefully opened the book. "I'd never seen a book so old, so of course, I had to go through it. It's filled with tales of vampires and..." she lowered her voice, "shifters."

She began to go through the pages slowly.

"Oh, I was wrong. The necklace isn't in the vampire part." She turned the book so I could see the page at the top where there was an image that looked like some kind of family crest. My heart started pounding when I saw the word *Atlandia* on the page. A chill slid down my spine.

"Ares told me a story about Atlandia. He said that there used to be a royal family over all the wolf packs in Europe. And they were wiped out not too long ago." For a second, images from the vision shot through my mind. Images of the castle. Of a king. Of a queen...

I shook my head, pushing the confusing thoughts away.

"Look, that's the necklace," Miyu said excitedly as she turned the page and pointed at a picture. And there the necklace was, featured prominently in the center of the page. I glanced down at the subtitle under the picture where it said that the necklace had belonged to the royal family for centuries. It had been said to hold magical powers that increased the strength of the royal dynasty and gave them special skills that set them apart from their subjects. The Atlandia royal family originated in Romania —the Carpathian Mountains more specifically.

I was just about to tell her about the strange experience I'd had when I'd touched the necklace, but all of a sudden, there was a loud crash just outside the room. It sounded like a wall had fallen down or something.

Daxon and Wilder sprang to their feet and ran towards the door.

"You've got to be fucking kidding me," Wilder growled.

And then all hell broke loose.

9

"Oh, fuck off," I growled.

I knew the fucker instantly by his putrid scent alone from when Rune had returned after he'd kidnapped her. He had tortured her, and I shook with fury at the memory. I was going to destroy Alistair. He'd better be prepared to cry because I was breaking one bone at a time so he felt every damned thing before I killed him.

The gutless prick stood behind his men just by the doorway...six bastards already in wolf form, and I had to admit...they were huge.

Humans were screaming and running out of the place from the other exits...as they should. Books dropped where they stood so they could escape.

I seethed, sucking in harsh breaths, seeing only red.

"Keep Rune safe," I shouted at Wilder, gaining myself a disdainful frown.

"Like fuck you're going to take them on by yourself."

Sure, he had a point. Seven against one...even I had to admit this might be over my head. But darkness consumed me.

"Fine." I turned to Rune quickly, calling out across the room. "Hide, sweetheart. I won't lose you again." She didn't seem to hear me as she was ushering Miyu to leave through the fire escape door at the rear of the room.

My heart pounded with excitement as I twisted towards the unwelcome visitors.

"Bickering like children," Alistair growled, shadows clinging to his ugly face. "Rune, come to me now, my fated mate. Or I'm going to kill both of the fuckheads you've let fuck you. You seem to forget I own you and your cunt."

Anger tore through me, his insults confirming his death for the hundredth time.

"You're gonna scream, asshole," I boomed, my wolf already pouring out of me brutally.

Wilder followed suit, changing into his black wolf, and perhaps the Moon Goddess was shining down on us because being the day after a full moon, a Lycan breed like him could still shift into his wolf. They got three days a month after the full moon. That was once again why a Bitten like me was superior. I controlled my wolf every damn day.

Falling onto all fours, white fur exploded across my body, clothes ripped to shreds. Bones cracked, limbs stretched, and hell, I loved the pain that came with a transformation. It felt like life.

Then I charged.

Fury swallowed me. It bled through my veins, fogging the corners of my mind with nothing but revenge for everything Alistair had ever done to my Rune.

*Hate...*the word formed into a stone in my gut, and it hardened with every step I took towards Alistair.

Three wolves came right for me, and I snarled my

threat, a heavy thunderous growl reverberating through my body.

Wilder pounced into the fight at my side, taking on his own three men, including Alistair, which pissed me off. The ass was mine to murder.

I slammed into the first wolf, our heads clashing. I felt no pain as I went berserk on them. Vicious snarls flooded the library, and I attacked with bared teeth, ripping at brown and grey fur, tearing into them. I spit out clumps of fur and flesh alike, pivoting left and right at my three opponents.

From the corner of my eye, I spotted Wilder smacking right into a wolf, sending it catapulting into the brick wall before the creature slumped to the floor like a pile of garbage.

I swung my attention back to my own party...three minions who came at me just as fast, and I was getting pissed. I lunged at the grey one and snatched him around the throat with my mouth just as another wolf crashed into my side. My back legs buckled for a split second, which was enough to release the wolf in my grip and send me sprawling onto my side. The third whacked into me too to ensure I fell off my feet.

My throat tightened and I hit the floorboards on my side, well aware this was the worst possible position to be in when surrounded by three enemies.

Gaping mouths, teeth bared...the wolves attacked.

Heart thudding in my chest, I threw out my back legs, kicking a fucker in the face, then scrambled to my feet as the other two fell onto me, biting, carving their fangs into me, sinking into flesh.

Growling, I went ballistic, swinging and attacking just as viciously, when another wolf from Wilder's side suddenly came flying in our direction, his body clubbing one of my attackers, completely wiping him out. Both were out cold.

Fuck yeah.

Using the window of opportunity, I leapt to my feet and faced my enemies. Blood seeped from the two wolves' bodies. They heaved for breath, fur raised on the back of their necks, ears flat against their heads. Piercing eyes locked on me.

And I charged towards them.

I rammed into the first wolf's ribs so hard that I drove him into one of the glass display cabinets with a Las Vegas feathery costume inside.

Glass shattered, the sound ear-piercing. Shards flew outward as the wolf broke right into the display, bringing the costume down with him. A plume of features burst upward from the golden outfit, looking like we'd just gone murder-crazy inside a chicken coop.

Wilder was pinned down under three wolves, while Alistair turned towards me, a blade raised in his hand. Asshole wasn't even in wolf form...what a prick, hiding behind his men.

Wilder's groans called to me, as did Rune's cries, calling his name.

I stared from him to Alistair and knew Rune would murder me if I let Wilder die.

Fuck me. Besides, he saved me earlier, so I owed him. One last glare at Alistair who was coming my way, and I swung towards Wilder.

Fury washed over me, and I crashed into the pile-up on Wilder, bringing them all off him. We broke into a massive brawl. I went feral.

It was only when I ripped into the neck of a wolf,

stealing his life away, that Rune's scream almost stopped my heart beating.

I jutted my head up, blood dripping over my chin, when I spotted her, cornered by one of the wolves. My heart constricted, and panic flared across my chest.

Wilder scrambled to his feet, snapping his jaws at two attackers.

Just then, a jolt of excruciating pain pierced my back leg, hurting like a fucking bitch. I flinched and twisted around to see Alistair jamming his blade into my thigh. I hollered with pain, shuddering.

The dick gave me his shit-eating grin that pulled across his face, wrinkling the corners of his eyes. Fucking assmunching sonofabitch.

"You're no match for me, pretty boy. I'm going to cut up your face then fuck you into hell."

Pretty boy? Thanks for noticing. I lunged at him, striking him faster than he expected by the sight of his bulging eyes. Good. He was about to feel what death felt like.

Flashes of fury blurred my vision, my pulse hammering in my veins. We hit the floor, him beneath me, all the while, Rune's screams bled into my ears.

My soul burned at hearing her cries, and the vision of her hurt.

Waiting wasn't going to work. Running on pure instinct, I followed my wolf, and I went to chomp down on Alistair's face. The bastard moved at the last minute.

My teeth sank right into his shoulder, so violently, I crunched down on bone and ripped away flesh and sinew. Blood spurted across my mouth...in my mouth.

He howled like a baby, but I ripped away from him and threw myself across the library.

I'm coming, sweetheart.

I bounded over tables, knocking over a huge book stand in the process, my sights set on Rune who was on the floor, pinned beneath a massive grey wolf. And rage rose through me like an inferno.

———

Rune

I screamed.

Dark wolf eyes glinted with malice, glaring down at me.

My gut squeezed, and I thrashed to escape the heavy paw pressed down on my chest, pinning me to the floor. Sharp tipped claws broke my skin, and I winced at the pain. All the while, drool seeped from the monster over me, dripping onto my chin. I wasn't sure if I wanted to keep screaming or hurl.

I called to my wolf as panic carved into me. I wouldn't go back to Alistair. I'd die before I let him touch me again because he'd torture me for the rest of my life—just to make his point that I wronged him.

Concentrating, I called to my wolf, my body tensing. Bile rose to the back of my throat with how hard I stiffened, pain flaring across my head. And when the warm trickle of blood seeped from my nose, I screamed out in pure frustration. I needed my wolf, and I was so tired of having her suppressed.

The huge wolf on top of me roared in my face, his breath a foul stink of something dead. His clawed paw dug into my chest. I drove my fists into him, my breaths short from barely being able to breathe thanks to the weight of his paw.

Just as quickly, he lashed forward, mouth parted, and grabbed me by the arm, teeth sinking into me.

I cried out, beating my fists into his head and chest as he started to drag me across the room.

I bucked and thrashed against him, praying to the Moon Goddess to give me back my wolf, knowing that I could destroy this asshole in a heartbeat.

And just as fast, he suddenly flew off me with a swoosh, a white blur attached to the wolf.

I peered at the fight, my gaze falling on Daxon in his white wolf form. I cried out a whimper from the pain in my arm, while my heart somersaulted, wanting him to end that dickhead.

Hope replaced my earlier fear, and I dragged myself to my feet, reaching for the nearest chair. I rushed after Daxon and the wolf he was rolling around with in a brawl. I whacked the chair into the monstrous brute.

He barely flinched, but it gave Daxon an upper hand. He threw him into a free-standing bookshelf so hard that it sent the whole thing falling backward. Which, of course, ended up in a domino effect, of the next shelf pushed over, and the next, until the entire row had been wrenched out of the floorboards they'd been secured to.

Yet Daxon and the enemy kept on fighting.

Blood.

Fur.

Chunks of flesh.

I swallowed hard at the sight because Daxon was literally biting pieces off him with such anger, it scared even me a bit. I wanted him to hurt these men though, to really bring them agony. Make them beg for salvation. Maybe I'd become sadistic since Alistair kidnapped me last, or maybe I just wanted justice for all the wrong he'd done to me.

Wilder roared, the sound so abrupt that I jumped in my skin and swept my attention over to him in the middle of the room. He tilted his head back, standing over a wolf torn in half at his feet. Blood pooled rapidly around the dead man, spreading like a tidal wave, seeping outward to swallow everything in its path.

The bitter smell of the pungent blood flooded the room, and trepidation trembled in my bones.

That was when I really took stock of the room. The dead wolves slowly morphed back into their human forms, blood splashed across the chairs and books, gaping holes in the walls.

And in the sweep, my gaze fell on Alistair, lingering in the exit doorway. He stared at me, giving me that dead, icy smile that promised retribution and all the pain he'd inflict on me. His eyes blazed with fire the longer he glared at me. I noticed one shoulder hung lower than the other, completely covered in blood.

In a heartbeat, he whipped around and vanished out of sight.

"Wilder," I cried out just as a terrifying screech had me snapping around to where Daxon had been.

It wasn't the best moment to have looked, in all honesty. The wolf Daxon had trapped against the fallen bookshelf cried like a dying animal just as my gorgeous man slashed his deadly claws along the wolf's neck. Over and over.

The spray of blood hit him and the books, then the wolf's head just snapped and rolled right off his shoulders.

I whimpered and looked away instantly, convinced I'd throw up. I was glad that I'd gotten Miyu out and she didn't have to see all of this. Except...we'd just destroyed her job. I'd have to make that up to her.

Wilder was at my side suddenly, in his human form... Naked, bleeding, and bruised. But he collected me into his arms, turning his back to the massacre, blocking it from my view.

"You're safe now," he growled, his voice gravelly and dark. "The wolves are all dead."

"Except for Alistair," I whispered. "The one who deserved to die."

"We'll get him, I promise, babe." Wilder rubbed my back in small circles. "Are you hurt?"

I shook my head. Deep inside, disappointment flared over me knowing that Alistair got away, and knowing that he'd be back for me. Cold danced down my spine at the thought, and I softened against Wilder.

He'd barely held me for a moment before a police siren rang in the distance, and I exchanged a worried look with Wilder. "We need to get out of here, now," he muttered. With a swing of his head behind him, he barked, "Daxon, enough. We have to leave."

Wilder grabbed a large, black coat he found on the floor near an overturned chair that must have belonged to one of the people who ran out of here screaming. He dragged it on, the fabric hitting mid-thigh, but it was large enough to fit... sort of. If you ignored the taut fabric across his biceps looking ready to burst open, resembling the Hulk.

It was at that same moment that something glinting in the fluorescent lights caught my attention from a pile of shredded clothes. Wilder's, more precisely, as I recognized the blue of his shirt. And in the pile, sat his car keys.

I reached down and snatched them.

Wilder then took my hand and we tore across the

destroyed library, swerving around turned tables, leaping over books. I lifted my gaze over my shoulder at the massacre the guys had left behind, noting Daxon had found a jacket he'd managed to fashion into a skirt around himself and chased after. He was splattered in blood, and people would freak out if they saw him.

On a different note, he looked more gladiator than wolf shifter. Yep, even as we bolted before the police found us with all these dead bodies, my libido reacted to my men. How could it not when I was surrounded by perfectly cut muscles. I loved seeing them naked.

We sprinted out of the library and swung left towards our car, drawing the attention of a few people nearby. Most were distracted by three cop cars speeding across the parking area, coming right for the building we'd burst out of.

We finally reached our car, and I frantically jumped into the driver's seat before jamming the keys into the ignition. I opened my window, spying Daxon pulling clothes out of the trunk of the car. They came prepared, it seemed. He tossed pants and a shirt to Wilder, and the pair rapidly dressed up in the shadow of our car, then both hopped into the back.

Of course, I burst out laughing as I knew exactly what they were thinking...that the other would drive, and I'd end up in the back with them.

"Hey," Wilder murmured, almost grumpy. "You were meant to be here with me."

"Time for you two to enjoy the back seat," I threw over my shoulder, noting that they were large enough to take up the seat completely, to the point where their legs actually touched. It was nice to find something funny considering we'd just been attacked.

"I don't like this," he said, while Daxon grumbled, both of them knocking shoulders in their attempt to get out.

Instead, I shoved the gear into drive and took off, saying, "Are either of you badly hurt?"

"Just scratches and bruises," Wilder said. "Though Daxon's bleeding badly from a hole in his leg."

"What? Daxon, you're hurt?" I slammed on the brakes and twisted around to face him, while he dragged his shirt off and folded it into a temporary bandage, before pressing it to the wound on the side of his thigh.

"I'm fine, sweetheart, and already feel myself healing. You focus on getting us out of here, okay?"

I nodded, and as much as I yearned to reach over and kiss away the pain I saw in his eyes, I had to get us away from the scene of the crime.

"Alistair must have eyes on us," Daxon mused, changing the conversation instantly. "How else would he have known we were at the library?"

"Maybe he followed my scent?" I suggested, figuring it sounded like the most logical reason. "Well, except that the fae curse is concealing it, so I don't really know how he found us."

Wilder's mouth thinned, the strain on his face most likely from his recent encounter with the fae queen putting a spell on him as well.

I licked my lips, taking a sharp turn quickly just as another police car zoomed past us, its siren ringing loudly, lights throbbing. I checked the rearview mirror constantly, but the police car wasn't turning around to come after us. We'd been driving for a solid fifteen minutes and no one chased after us, so I took that as a clean getaway.

I pulled out my phone and texted Miyu to make sure

she was okay and apologizing for the chaos that seemed to follow me everywhere.

That was crazy, she replied. *And don't worry about the job, I hated that place. I miss doing hair.*

Will you come back? I texted, holding my breath for her answer.

Eventually, she responded. *I think I still need more time. But I'll keep in touch.*

I bit my lip and nodded to myself. Hopefully with the happiness I'd pushed into her, and a little bit of time, she would be okay.

"Been thinking that we need to pay Daria a visit. She needs to die," Wilder suggested out of the blue, drawing my attention back. "It's the only way I can think to remove your fae curse, Rune. You'll get your wolf and strength back."

"And how do you kill a fae?" I asked, keeping my eyes on the traffic.

"Iron is poisonous to them," Daxon answered. "If there's enough of it in their body, it will slowly start weakening them, making them sick until they pass away."

"I have no idea how we're supposed to manage that," I answered.

"There's another way. Driving an iron blade into their heart and leaving it embedded."

"That could work," Daxon stated, looking slightly pale as he held the fabric to his wound. Blood smeared across his cheek and neck, and he looked exhausted—face pale, shadows darkening under his eyes.

Wilder, on the other hand, stared outside the window, looking lost in thought.

Eradicating someone as powerful as Daria would not be

an easy feat or I'm sure someone would have done it already.

Especially Wilder.

But to have my curse removed would be incredible, and I wanted to release my wolf after she'd been locked up all this time.

My thoughts flew to Ares' blue stone on his necklace, and his insistence that if we found the second half of the artifact, it would remove the curse as well. Did I trust Ares? Was he telling the truth?

A loud ring sounded from the middle console near me, and I flinched at the abrupt sound. I glanced down to find a buzzing cell phone just as Wilder stuck his hand forward and grabbed it.

Seriously, I almost jumped out of my skin. I was so on edge.

"Yeah," he answered.

I kept looking at him through the mirror as he nodded and made small sounds in his throat. His brow furrowed, then he muttered, "What the fuck for?"

The way he said that made my stomach clench.

Even Daxon was curious, staring at Wilder for some kind of explanation.

Silence followed, then Wider stated, "Fine. We'll be there before nightfall." Then he hung up and tossed the phone back into the middle console.

"What the fuck now?" Daxon asked.

With a hard breath, he said, "Louis, the alpha's brother from the Blood Pack, has made an unexpected visit to Amarok to speak with us."

"What the hell for?" Daxon pushed forward, his shoulders aggressively lifting. "Last time we encountered him, he threatened to take our land and packs from us. You should have let me slice his tongue on his last visit."

"Shut the hell up," Wilder snapped, rubbing his temple. "The past is just that. But we need to get back there fast and deal with this shit now, then we need to fix up Rune's curse."

"Who in the world is the Blood Pack?" I asked.

"Assholes," Daxon blurted out.

"One of our neighboring packs who we've never seen eye to eye with on anything," Wilder explained, his voice tight. He glanced back out the window and never continued his explanation.

Well, that was great. Because we didn't have enough enemies.

10

DAXON

"There's nothing on earth quite as delicious as you, sweetheart," I whispered in Rune's ear as I carried her to bed.

Halfway through the drive home, I took over driving in order to give Rune a break. The sweet thing ended up falling asleep from exhaustion. I couldn't blame her after everything she'd gone through.

I was so fucking tired of Alistair. It made me crazy to have him running around, and once again unable to do anything about it.

Rune frowned in her sleep and I softly stroked her cheek until her face relaxed. She was a precious little morsel and all mine. Well...mine and Wilder's. I knew I had it bad when I'd accepted that.

Look at me...having a threesome with the fucking guy. But for her, I'd do anything.

I cradled her soft body in my arms, pressed tight to my chest, and it took all my strength to not just climb into bed with her. To hell with the Blood Pack. I hated politics and drama...that was Wilder's skill. He knew how to control a room. While I had zero patience and preferred to cut the throats of anyone who annoyed me.

"Did you read that somewhere?" Rune croaked, opening her eyes and smiling. When she looked at me that way, I felt invincible. To have someone as perfect and good as her actually love someone like me was a miracle. I wasn't the easiest person to get along with. Not the nicest either. Yet, she saw past my ugly parts.

"So, you're awake after all. Is this your way of making me carry you inside?" Of course, I'd carry her even if she was full of energy. I loved the way she felt against my body, and how I bathed in her scent, and it gave me ample opportunity to keep her by my side.

She laughed softly and made no effort to pull out of my arms. "Being carried is a form of being worshipped, you know?"

I held her tighter as I entered my bedroom and crossed the dark room. "You *are* my goddess, so it makes sense. I'll lay at your feet anytime, and I assure you that you'll love every second of it. I'll give you everything and hold nothing back. You are my universe."

Even in the semi-darkness, I watched the faint blush darken across her cheeks. After all our time together, I loved how sincere and vulnerable she remained.

"You make me swoon with the things you say. Things I would have never imagined you saying, and now you're melting me."

I laid her on my bed gently and sat by her side. Moonlight streamed in from the window across her gorgeous face, and she yawned.

"I'll come join you as soon as I can, but I need to help Wilder real quick." I brushed fingertips across her brow, pushing her blonde hair off her face. I moved my hands down to her shirt to pull it off her and get her tucked into bed.

She laughed and brushed my hand away. "Nice try, buddy. You better go as Wilder will be waiting for you. I'm fine. I'm going to crash. Now off you go." She playfully pushed me away, and I knew she was right. The moment her clothes came off, I'd end up fucking her all night.

I chuckled. "You got me there." I leaned over and kissed her on the mouth, then pulled back and went into my closet to get changed out of my blood-stained clothes.

The knife wound had mostly closed up, the blood coagulated, and by tomorrow would resemble a bruise.

By the time I changed into jeans and dragged on a button-up shirt, Rune was breathing heavily, already fast asleep.

I turned to study her where she lay curled up on her side, looking beautiful. It hurt my soul to think that Alistair thrived off hurting her, when she deserved to be told she was a queen every single day. She deserved love, loyalty, and a lot of orgasms.

Smiling to myself, I was already thinking of returning to my room later on and crawling in next to her. Fuck, everything about her clouded my mind.

Unable to help myself, I stepped next to the bed and ran my knuckles gently across her cheek. She made a small, inviting sound that made me hard at the thought of her moaning beneath me. Her scent flooded my nostrils and I breathed her deeper. She was fucking intoxicating, and every instinct pushed me to strip her curvy body, spread her legs, and leave a trail of kisses down her inner thighs before drawing her little clit into my mouth, sucking on her until she screamed.

Heading outside, I made a quick pace across the

grounds to the cafe, where Mr. Jones had cleared out the place for our meeting. Wilder insisted on a more casual setting, convinced it might encourage a quicker conversation.

If you asked me, I'd have met him on the side of the road and demanded that he tell me what he wanted before I slit his throat. Did I mention that I fucking hated these bull-shit suck-up meetings? The only reason Wilder wanted me there was for sheer support in case shit went sideways. I certainly wasn't the ambassador of the two of us.

It was hard to concentrate with how furious I still was about Alistair's attack today, and how the fuck he tracked us down to the library in Las Vegas. Did he have someone tailing us everywhere we went? The notion had my hackles bristling.

Marching up the street, I instantly spotted four suits standing outside the cafe...Blood Pack's muscle, I guessed.

I marched right inside without acknowledging them, my gaze instantly fastening on Wilder and Louis, the pack alpha's brother. They sat at the round table in the middle of the empty cafe. Louis was a round man with matching cheeks and head. Bald as a bowling ball, he always dressed immaculately in Ermenegildo Zegna suits, looking every part the epitome of a mafia godfather. Maybe that had been his intention, or the whole sharing the alpha status with his brother thing, had gone to his fat head.

"Daxon," Wilder stated, almost sounding relieved to have me join them.

Louis got to his feet, and I nodded my acknowledge-ment, while he stretched out his hand. "It's been too long, Daxon." He eyed me up and down, then paused on the side of my face. "I see you're still fighting your own battles instead of delegating."

"I'm a big believer in leading by example." I accepted his hand, squeezing hard as I shook it. We were wolves who bared teeth to show dominance, and yet here we were playing nice, shaking hands, and serving him fucking coffee.

Not showing a sign of pain from me practically constricting the life out of his hand, he grinned, showing me his teeth finally. Ah, and there was his wolf. Good, now we were on the same playing field and not this pretend bullshit.

According to Wilder, I had to resist killing him tonight. He wanted Louis out of there as fast as possible, while not declaring war with another large pack, so I'd do my best. But, I hated this guy. He hunted down animals and kept their heads hanging on his walls as trophies and for bragging rights. And I wasn't talking about rabbits, but large prey, including a few human skulls.

I just wanted this bullshit done. After all, I had a goddess in my bed, and I didn't have plans to leave her alone for too long.

"What gives us the honor of your visit?" I asked, trying my best to sound as pompous as him. He released my hand, and we took our seats around the table. Wilder to my left, and Louis across from me.

Mr. Jones took that as the cue to hurry out with his tray of coffees and assorted treats. The poor sucker looked nervous, his hands shaking, and he kept his gaze low, not looking any of us in the eye. No doubt that would have been at Wilder's instructions.

Louis stirred sugar into his coffee, then took a sip before exhaling loudly and letting his shoulders drop.

"We haven't always seen eye to eye on things, but I think we're at a crossroads right now, where we are better

off forming an alliance rather than being the opposition."
Louis reached for a chocolate brownie and popped it into
his mouth.

"And why would we do that?" Wilder asked exactly
what I was thinking.

"You see, we have a new enemy in this part of the country. An alpha who's been attacking other packs, including
my wolves. He has one goal—take ownership of all our packs
and form one overpowering army where we all report to
him. Oppose him, and he'll slaughter you."

I blinked at Louis as he smacked his lips. If I didn't
know better, I'd say he was scared of this newcomer.

"And you think there's more strength in joining our
forces," Wilder filled in the unsaid words.

"Exactly. You have two large packs. My men are some of
the most powerful in the country, so we'd be unstoppable
together."

I half-choked on my breath at his statement, and he
glanced over at me, unimpressed. "Is something funny?"

Wilder turned his head towards me as well, his features
twisted into a wry warning for me to keep my mouth shut.
Wouldn't it be easier to tell the guy to go fuck himself?

Instead, I reined it in. "Nothing at all," I gripped. "Now,
you were going to tell us who this big bad alpha in town is."

Louis shifted in his seat, tightness capturing his lips, a
light growl playing on his throat. He turned his attention to
Wilder. "He goes by the name Alistair."

Instantly, my shoulders reared back at hearing that
name. And I wasn't the only one. Wilder stiffened, his eyes
large.

"So, you've heard of him too," Louis stated, not seem-
ingly surprised.

"Something like that," Wilder answered.

I was practically gripping the table, ready to toss it aside and force this dickhead to tell me everything he knew about Alistair. "Okay, so we're listening. What do you know about him? Where's he staying?"

Louis smirked, and if he thought for a second that he had an upper hand over me because I was suddenly interested, he had a rude awakening coming his way.

"The guy's a slimy bastard," Wilder stated. "But what do you want us to do?"

"Join forces. We share information on where Alistair and his men are. Then we take him out."

I narrowed my eyes on Louis, well aware of how much of a dickhead Alistair was, but it surprised me this wolf was at our door asking for our help. "Didn't you just finish telling us you had some of the strongest wolves in your pack? What can we possibly do to help you?"

By Wilder's sharp glare, he wasn't a fan of my question, but I was still irritated by this guy being in our home and stealing my time away from Rune.

Taking a long drink from his coffee, he set it back on the table and licked his lips, throwing daggers at me. "Thing is, the encounters we've had with him should have eliminated him, but somehow he always manages to survive and escape. And then he returns with twice as many wolves. I've already lost half a dozen wolves to him. Including two females stolen right out of their homes, and I still haven't found them."

The strain at the corner of his mouth showed, and his real reason for coming to us became clear. He was desperate. My gut tightened as a surge of concern tore through my veins. Today was an example of Alistair sneaking up on us, then escaping. He didn't give a shit about his men, that was clear.

"We have a mutual enemy," Louis continued. "If your family was in danger, wouldn't you do anything to protect them?"

I held his stare, and he looked away first, then turned his attention to Wilder.

"This will benefit us all. My brother and I have a lot of connections that could be of use for you."

"Do you know where he's staying?" Wilder asked.

Louis shook his head. "He moves constantly, from what I've managed to work out. I have scouts everywhere, watching for him and his men. But somehow he always knows where we are, surprising us with attacks."

Interest piqued further, I leaned in closer, while Wilder asked, "Tell me more about exactly where he attacked you, how many wolves he had with him. Everything to see if there's a pattern."

Louis eyed us both. "So, that's an agreement to an alliance? We'll need a blood truce to agree there will be no killing between our packs."

A growl rolled over my throat, which Wilder ignored, while Louis picked up on it with the way he stared my way. His gaze screamed predator, but we also had a chance to gain more information on Alistair and finally fuck him up.

"Agreed," Wilder instantly accepted. Maybe he was onto something. Get information from him first, then cut their throats and be done with it. The thought did put me in a good mood, so I happily agreed and we shook on it.

Louis' lips parted with a heavy inhale, then broke into a detailed explanation of every location they'd encountered Alistair, while Wilder and I hung on every word.

One way or another, we were killing Alistair. Even if it meant appeasing our enemies...for now.

———

Rune

I moaned as I sunk into the warm water, vanilla and coconut brushing against my senses from the fragrant bath oil floating on the surface. A bubble landed on my nose, and I reached out my hand to brush it away.

"This was just what I needed," I purred contentedly.

"I'll always give you what you need," a familiar voice answered. My eyes flew open in shock when I saw Ares leaning back on the other side of the tub, grinning wickedly at me.

I immediately yelped and pulled my knees up to my chest, grateful for all the bubbles in the water so he couldn't see any important parts. My gaze flicked around the bathroom, not recognizing anything about it. I glanced back to Ares and gave him my best glare.

"What did you do?" I growled.

His hair was wet and hanging around his face in a way that looked far too sexy. His chiseled chest was out of the water, drops of liquid trailing down his skin like he'd been underneath the surface and had just popped out. I wasn't going to admit how hard it was to keep my eyes just on his face.

"I didn't do anything," he said innocently, shrugging his shoulders. "This is your dream."

"I'm dreaming?" I asked, feeling a little bit of relief. Because I didn't think he was lying. There was a certain perfection about our surroundings that made me think he was telling the truth. The water was the perfect temperature, and everything in the unfamiliar bathroom was so pretty it was practically sparkling. Glancing around, I would swear that there was a glittery haze surrounding us.

"Get out of my dream," I ordered crossly.

He chuckled and put his arms behind his head, leaning back and showcasing the strength of his arms.

I went a little slack-jawed at the sight before quickly shaking my head to try and snap myself out of it. I began pinching my arm.

"What are you doing?" he asked with a laugh.

"Trying to wake myself up."

I blinked, and all of a sudden, he was behind me in the tub, and I was reclining against his hard chest, his erect length sitting right under my ass.

"Why don't you just enjoy yourself, *Dragostea mea*," he murmured, his breath brushing against my skin.

I squeaked and tried to pull away, but then his arms were wrapping around me, holding me close.

"Let me go!" I hated how halfhearted my voice sounded.

He stroked his fingers across my stomach softly, sending shivers across my skin despite the fact that we were in warm water. His other hand began to massage the base of my scalp, and it was like he'd found a magic button, because I felt my entire body relaxing against him.

"That's it, my heart. Just relax. I've missed you every second that we've been apart."

"I guess this means you lived," I murmured, a moan in my voice from how good I felt under his ministrations.

"I know you're happy about that, *Dragostea mea*."

"What language is that?" I asked, deliberately ignoring his statement and how right it was.

"Romanian," he answered as he loosened his arm a bit. I'd lost my mind, because I made no attempt to pull away.

"What does that mean?"

He nuzzled against my hair, breathing me in. "My love. My darling. My beloved."

Fireworks started to shoot off in my insides. Why did he have to be so fucking charming?

I tried to keep the image of him about to feed on me central in my brain, but the image felt slippery. Every time I tried to focus on it, my mind would drift to some sweet thing he'd done or said in the short time that I'd known him.

"How are you able to do this?" I moaned. Both of his hands were now kneading my shoulders, and there had to be some kind of magic involved, because no massage I'd ever received had ever felt like this.

"We can always visit each other's dreams. It's a blood match gift."

I wrinkled my nose. There was that stupid word again.

I decided to change the subject.

"We found a book about that necklace in a library in Las Vegas. But it didn't exactly give many details about where to find the other half."

"I'm not quite sure about that either," he said disappointedly.

"The book we found said that it belonged to the royal family you told me about." Ares hummed but didn't say anything.

"You still haven't told me how my family hurt yours. Does the necklace have something to do with that?"

"You're asking far too many questions. You're supposed to be relaxing," he answered, before moving one of his hands from my shoulder, sliding between my breasts, and heading straight to my clit. I jumped as he began to play my body like he knew it intimately. Something in my head urged me to move away, but for the life of me, I couldn't think what it was. A pleased moan slipped from my lips as his other hand moved from my shoulder to my breasts. He began to knead them softly, before playing with my nipple. My body bucked, but his finger never strayed from that sweet spot he was hitting on my clit. I could feel an orgasm building up inside of me as he stroked a finger through my folds.

He abruptly moved his hands, and I cried out as he chuckled darkly.

"I'm going to take care of you, my heart," he promised, reaching to the side of the tub and grabbing a fancy bottle of bath wash and a loofah. He squeezed the bath wash onto the sponge and then began to wash me, sliding his hands all over my body just as much as he used the loofah. His strokes were long and slow, and my breath was coming out in gasps as he continued to turn me on.

"Feeling relaxed?"

I moaned in response and then he was pushing two fingers into me, working them in and out and finding that spot inside that made me fall apart.

"Ares," I moaned, and then he began to drag his sharp incisors down my neck softly, sending tingles racing across my skin.

"I'm desperate to taste you," he purred. "Don't you want that?"

Suddenly, he licked my face. And then he licked it again.

I shot up in my bed, staring around the dark room wildly. My body was on fire, but I definitely wasn't in a bathtub. And I was dry....except for my cheek. It was wet, and a bit slimy...what the fuck?

My heart began to race as a low growl filled the dark room.

"Daxon?" I asked in a trembling voice, hoping he was playing some sort of awful joke on me because the alternative was much worse. I was still in Daxon's house, so I guess that was at least good.

The growls grew louder. It was like I was surrounded by creatures. As much as I would've loved to jump off my bed and run out of the room, nowhere seemed safe.

Then, out of the shadows, it appeared. The monster I'd seen in the woods. It was enormous, with red eyes that glowed in the darkness. The razor-sharp spikes running down its spine stood at attention, and when it opened its mouth, I could see serrated teeth.

We stared at each other, my heart racing so fast and so loud in my chest that I was sure the creature could hear it.

It dropped back on its haunches like he was about to lunge, and then it surged forward. I closed my eyes and prepared to feel its teeth and claws ripping into my skin...

And then a warm, rough tongue licked up the side of my face and the bed sank down in front of me.

"What?" I gasped as it did it again. I slowly opened my eyes, still expecting to be attacked, and saw the giant beast on the bed, his tongue hanging out of its mouth as it huffed loud breaths...just like a dog.

I stared at it incredulously. It barked at me—well I assumed it was a bark. It sounded far more monstrous and menacing than a dog ever would, but there was still a playful tinge to it.

He leaned forward and licked my hand that I was still holding out in front of me to protect myself. As soon as I felt his tongue, I yanked my hand away and the beast whined.

"I've got to still be dreaming," I murmured. The creature whined again and pressed its wet nose against my leg, like it wanted something.

"What do you want?" I snapped, and its answering sad whine made me feel guilty.

It nudged my leg again and then laid its monstrous head on my leg and stared up at me with its red eyes balefully.

"Do you want me to pet you?" I asked, feeling like an idiot that I was even having that thought. Why would the monster-dog want me to pet it?

I jumped when he barked happily in response. Well then.

"You're not going to bite me, right?" I asked, very much aware that my sanity had cracked and now I was talking to this creature like it was an oversized puppy.

It whined again and I took that to be a good sign. I reached out tentatively, with a trembling hand as I passed over its snout with its terrifying teeth, past its red glowing eyes, and onto his head. I flinched and ripped my hand away when it barked again. But then he lunged forward and licked my face twice more. His breath was fucking awful. I reached out again and this time allowed myself to pet his head. His fur was coarse and wiry, but he seemed to enjoy my touch because he started purring... loudly.

"Wake up, Rune," I ordered myself. First I'd been having sex dreams about Ares while lying in Daxon's bed, and now I was dreaming that the terrifying monster in the woods was actually an oversized dog and wanted to be my new best friend.

No more eating cheese right before bed, I decided.

The beast seemed really sweet though. At least it did right at that moment. He was inching forward as I petted him until he was half laying on my lap, cutting off my circulation because he was so damn big.

"Are you a good boy?" I found myself cooing, and he

purred loudly in response. Abruptly, he jumped away from me and off the bed. And then he started to run around in circles...chasing his spiked tail. The whole room was shaking as he ran, the pictures on the walls rattling. I didn't know where Daxon and Wilder were, but they couldn't have been close if they weren't running into the room right now after hearing this commotion.

The beast chased its tail for a few more seconds before sitting back on his haunches and cocking his head as he looked at me curiously. I didn't know how a monster could look at you curiously with bright red eyes, but it was definitely happening.

When I didn't seem to have anything to say, it settled on the ground with a loud thump and then began to promptly gnaw on the wooden foot of the bed. Its teeth were as razor-sharp as I'd thought, because it only took a few moments before the front of the bed was crashing down because he'd broken through the wood.

It lifted its head up from the post and stared at me like it was making sure I wasn't mad, but I was too shocked to do anything. When it started to rip into the mattress next, I jumped up.

"No," I said sternly, and it whined and backed away from the bed, his ears drooping sadly.

I felt a little sad for yelling at the ugly thing.

But that seemed stupid. "Leave," I tried next, but it just whined and settled onto the floor, not taking its eyes off me for a second.

I looked around the room, wondering how it had even gotten in here in the first place.

And what the fuck was I going to do about it?

I somehow needed to get it outside before Wilder and Daxon saw it. Because they would definitely try to kill it, and judging by how it was acting right now...that was probably not necessary.

Besides saving it, I was probably saving Wilder and Daxon from some serious bodily injury as well. It was very possible that it could be cute and cuddly one minute, and then attack anyone the next second when they tried to cause it harm.

I slipped off the bed, keeping my eyes locked with the beast's. I didn't think turning my back on it was a smart idea.

My window was closed, and it was far too small to fit the creature anyway, so I'd have to get it out of the house through the doors.

Unlike what had happened with Ares, I was pretty positive this was not a dream and was definitely currently happening.

What was my life?

At that moment, the creature sat up, lifted its leg, and started peeing the most foul-smelling urine I'd ever smelled.

And it wasn't just a trickle, it was a deluge that quickly soaked the floor.

Perfect. This was just getting better and better. I was not touching that.

I slipped on my house slippers and carefully walked around the large puddle he'd created on the floor. Then I started backpedaling to the door so I could keep him in my sights. He tracked my movements, his spiky tail banging against the floor as he feverishly wagged it.

"Come here, boy," I whispered as I reached behind me and quietly turned the doorknob. "Let's get you out of here."

He leaped to his feet and dashed towards me, almost barreling me over.

"That's a good boy," I said in the ridiculous baby voice I'd found myself adopting. I opened the door wider and stepped backwards, trying to keep one eye on my new monster pet and the other searching for any sign that the guys were around.

I spied movement on the back patio and saw that Daxon and Wilder were sitting in the outdoor chairs, on the deck, drinking beers. It was still weird to see the little bromance they seemed to be reluctantly developing.

The creature yipped and my attention went back to it. He was seated back on his haunches, his tongue hanging out of his terrifying mouth, just staring at me expectantly.

"Keep following me," I cooed, making my way through the house towards the front door. At one point the beast lifted his leg again. "No," I ordered in a panic, knowing that I definitely didn't want Daxon's antique table to have monster pee all over it.

Somehow we made it to the front door.

"Sit," I tried, and to my surprise, he listened. What was this thing? He almost seemed...trained.

I opened the door and peered out, making sure there wasn't anyone around. Daxon's house was off by itself, but since he was alpha you never knew when someone was going to drop by with a problem they wanted him to solve. When I saw that the coast was clear, I walked outside, ordering the monster to follow me.

Now that I'd made it this far, I wasn't sure what I was supposed to do. Order him to leave and not eat anyone? I could hear Daxon and Wilder's voices in my head telling me that he needed to be put down, but that was definitely not happening.

The sliding glass door in the back slid open and I quickly closed the front door behind me. They'd be out here any minute seeing what I was doing.

"You have to go home. And you're not going to touch anyone, okay?" I asked.

The monster licked my face in response.

"Blah," I gasped, wiping the slobber off my face. I didn't know if I was ever going to feel clean again after this. I pointed out to the forest. "Go home!"

He whined and looked at the forest and then back at me, his posture drooping.

"You're not in trouble. You just can't stay here," I said soothingly, a weird part of me wishing I could keep him.

The beast whined again. I reached over and scratched his head softly. Footsteps came closer to the front door from inside.

The beast finally stepped off the front porch and began to lope into the forest, just as the front door opened and Daxon appeared in the doorway.

"What are you doing out here?" he asked, looking around suspiciously.

"I was sending my pet home," I said, pushing past him into the house. "I'm going to need a mop and a bucket."

11

WILDER

The air knocked out of me at the sight of Rune, her blonde hair seeming to glow in the morning sunlight.

She was jogging around the town field not too far behind Daxon's home for her morning run. I felt like a pervert, because all I could stare at were her bouncing breasts, those long, trim legs, and her delicious ass moving with each step.

My first instinct was to chase after her, pin her down to the ground, and strip her. I was an animal like that, and I'd woken up with the world's biggest hard-on, and Rune on my mind. Not finding her in her bed, I tracked her down to the field.

Daxon had gone to work at the diner, while we had the Betas positioned all around the town for any intruders. Especially Alistair. After the eye-opening discussion with Louis two nights ago, it became apparent that Alistair has been a lot more active in this part of the country lately. I suspected it had everything to do with him getting Rune back...or making her suffer. Perhaps both. Either way, I had my men out scouting all the locations Alistair had been seen in the last couple of days. I intended to find him first and take him down before he grew his followers.

Turning my attention back to my beautiful girl, I studied the sunlight beaming down on her shoulders, blonde hair pulled into a ponytail and swinging wildly across her back.

Once she finished, I intended to take her out for breakfast and try to bring some kind of calmness into her life. She'd been through so much, and I noticed how easily she jumped at any sound. I'd do anything to put her at ease.

She noticed me then, and I watched as she pivoted in my direction, giving me the perfect view of the way her fucking perfect tits bounced as she moved. My cock stiffened in my pants. I combed a hand through my hair and blew out a long exhale to somehow get my mind off the obvious hunger stirring within me.

We'd been rushing around like mad lately, and well, I still wasn't settled with how often Daxon got to screw Rune. I still couldn't believe he'd joined in when I'd fucked her by the side of the road. Daxon was obsessed, and he couldn't keep his hands off her. And I intended to make sure he didn't fuck her more than me.

The closer she got, the more my dick twitched.

She finally reached my side with a huge smile, perspiration pebbling across her brow, and she breathed heavily. "I'm badly out of shape," she huffed. "I need to start running daily again. Maybe you can join me." That grin of hers was wicked.

"Maybe," I answered, my voice hoarse.

"Anyway, what's going on? Did something happen?" She was stretching her calf muscles, wearing Lycra shorts and a matching tank top that followed every delicious curve. Did she realize how hard it was to stare at her and not trip over myself because of how sexy she looked?

"I couldn't find you in your room so I came to search for you," I murmured truthfully, already reaching out to take her hand into mine. Her skin was cool to the touch, slightly damp. And when I inhaled, I breathed in her perspiration mingled with the sex scent that called to me. I gave up on breakfast plans for the time being and drew her into a walk back to the house.

I wasn't going to last the day if I didn't plunge my cock into her right now.

"I haven't finished running," she said, staring at me confused. "Where are we going?"

"We're going to fuck," I answered sincerely.

She choked on her next breath, and I laughed at how adorable she was at not knowing how crazy she drove us. If I had things my way, I'd fill her pussy with my cock every night before she fell asleep in my arms, and then I'd wake her up the same way.

"You don't believe in mincing your words." Still, she kept up with me and wasn't pulling away.

I paused and brought her against me, our bodies pressed against each other, my cock hardening at having her so close. "You know I'll take care of you, sweetheart. But I have needs that are strangling me. Just looking at you is killing me. Hell, I dreamt last night of your lips around my cock, and I woke up still feeling the flat of your tongue dragging over my erection. I'm so fucking hard for you."

The corners of her mouth curved upward, and there was no hesitation as she slid her hand between us. Her fingers curled over the bulge in my pants, and I hissed at her touch, at the way she lightly squeezed me.

"Fuck, Rune." I shuddered beneath her.

"You want me to suck your cock?" she purred the words, then unzipped my jeans.

My heart thundered, and when she slipped her hand into my jeans, wrapping her fingers around my shaft, I snarled, half-convinced I'd explode any second now. "Babe, you have no idea what you're doing to me. You're always on my mind, and I think about fucking you dozens of times a day, about sinking into your cunt."

Her hand moved up and down, and I ran my hand through her hair, fisting it. "You're such a good girl for me, aren't you?"

But then I caught movement across the river. If I could see them making their way to the main road, then they could see me.

I took her hand out of my pants, quickly guiding her toward the house. "Not here," I answered, practically running inside with her.

We were barely past the door when I grabbed her pants and wrenched them down her legs. Her scent engulfed me, and if I thought I was a lost cause to her before, well, I'd just lost my mind.

"I should probably have a shower first," she murmured. "I'm all sweaty."

"I love your scent and there's no time for a shower. I need you now."

She gasped. Then, as if understanding my complete lack of patience, she ripped off her tank top and bra and stood in front of me completely naked... well, with the exception of her sneakers. Perky breasts tipped with pink, hardened nipples, and smooth skin between the apex of her thighs demanded my attention.

"I love it when you're so horny," she muttered, licking

her lips while tugging my jeans down to my ankles. I tore off my t-shirt just as she shoved my cock into her mouth.

The force with which she took me slightly surprised me.

"Mmm, yes. Such a precious love you are. Now, go deeper." My fingers pushed through her hair and to the back of her head, guiding her deeper.

She looked up at me, and the sight of my huge cock sliding in and out of her mouth was breathtaking. Her hands rested against my thighs, helping her to keep her balance as she worked me deeper into her mouth until I kissed the back of her throat. She choked at first, her eyes watering, but she never paused.

I loved watching the way she worked me with her mouth, the flat pad of her tongue dragging over the base of my dick. Goddess, she was going to kill me.

"Your beautiful mouth is made for my cock," I groaned, knowing if she continued, I'd unload down Rune's throat. And I was dying to fuck her hard, to ram into that tight pussy.

I drew out of her mouth, much to her protesting moan. Then I stepped out of my jeans and threw them onto the couch.

She stared at me with such sadness, I swooped my gorgeous girl up and into my arms. "Don't worry, we're not even close to being done. But I need to fuck you because your cunt is so much better."

"I love the way you feel in my mouth. So hard, and you taste so good."

"You've ruined me for life, you know that?" I set her down at the side of the couch and turned her around to face away from me.

"Bend over for me, gorgeous." I gently ran my hand up the length of her back, pushing her forward over the armrest. "I want to see your drenched, pink pussy in the air."

She didn't protest, but she shivered beneath my touch. She smelled of heady sex, her arousal deepening. Leaning over the couch with her ass lifted, she glanced at me with eyes that were almost glazed over, glittering with desire.

"Is this what you want?" she asked, flirting with her voice.

"You have no idea how gorgeous you are. If you could see my view...fuck me, Rune. Your hot little pussy is dripping for me, but I'm going to make it drip with my cum." Nudging her legs apart wider, I stepped between them and pressed my cock to that perfect entrance.

She was on fire, and before I even pushed inside, she moaned, lifting her hips higher. The horny little thing was dying for my cock.

"Are you ready?" But before she could respond, I rammed into her.

She screamed beautifully, like a song to my ears, her body arching. I held on so she didn't slip forward and out of my reach.

I fucked Rune hard, sliding in and out of that tight core, my hips rocking fast. "You're fucking amazing," I growled as she moaned louder, and all I could think about was how tightly she squeezed my cock.

A glint of something off to my right caught my attention. It happened to be the full-length mirror from the bathroom, just past the open door. It was perfectly in line with us, and the view was spectacular. Bent over, her ass jiggling each time I slammed into her. It made me harder just watching us.

"Look to your right, baby," I ordered her. "Can you see me fucking you in the mirror?"

She twisted her head, and I saw her eyes pinned on us in our reflection. "It looks so hot."

I plunged quicker into her drenched hole, arousal trickling down the insides of her legs. And we watched each other, me claiming her body, over and over. Balancing her hands on the cushions, she pushed her ass back against each of my assaults, deepening my thrusts.

"Oh, babe," I ground out, my voice a dark cry.

"Please, more," she called out, her walls starting to constrict me, and she grew closer.

It was at that same moment that my cell phone, still in my jeans, rang. "Answer it," I growled, still hammering into her.

"What, not now," she mewled between catching her breath.

"Rune, get it just in case it's an update from my men." She felt too incredible to stop.

She pawed for my jeans, finally pulling out the phone.

Daxon's name flashed across the screen, and I smirked.

"I can't answer this," she moaned.

"Rune, pick it up," I commanded, barely holding on. I ran my thumb across her soaking wet ass crack, playing with her tight little hole, her body starting to shudder.

She hit answer on the phone, just as I pushed a finger into her, and her attempt to say hello morphed into a delicious scream of arousal. She cried out, an orgasm tearing through her gorgeous body, shaking in my arms as her pussy clamped down on my cock, milking me, bringing forward my own climax.

I growled, ramming into her one last time as I burst inside her, filling her with my seed. Our bodies were morphed into a harmony of bliss.

Just then, Daxon's abrupt, grizzly voice roared over the phone, "Wilder, you fucking asshole." Then he hung up.

Rune finally calmed down and slumped in front of me, sucking in long breaths, and I pulled out of her. I stepped back and admired my handiwork. "I love seeing you like this. Your pussy swollen and my cum dripping out. Fucking beautiful." I lifted her from the hips and drew her into the bathroom by the hand. "Let me wash you."

Her cheeks were flushed, and she smiled. "You need to do that more often. It was incredible. Well, except for the teasing Daxon part. He's going to be so pissed."

I laughed, satisfied that he understood how it felt to be teased to the point it hurt.

Daxon

"You sure this is the place?" I asked, staring at a field of pine trees on either side of the road. There was no way this could be Alistair's hideout; there were barely any cars here.

"My informants said they'd seen him traveling this road the three times they spotted him. So, if he's using this direction to reach our packs and others nearby, then he's got to be hiding out here."

"I guess, but fuck. What's he got? A treehouse?" I laughed at how ridiculous that sounded. "I'll keep my eyes peeled for anything."

Half an hour later, I blinked at the woods, when we zipped right past a rough track to our right. "Slow down, there's something back there." I craned my neck to glance back at it, when Wilder swerved like a madman, doing a tight U-turn across the double-laned road.

I whacked the side of my head into my window from how abruptly he turned, our tires screeching against the asphalt.

My stomach rose as though I rode a rollercoaster, and an excited adrenaline roared through me. I howled, loving how fast we spun, all while Wilder madly worked the steering wheel to keep us in control.

Coming to a sudden stop in the middle of the lane, I burst out laughing. "Man, I had no idea you had it in you to have fun."

Breathing hard, he checked his mirrors and took off going back the way we'd come, and I noticed he was slightly shaken. "I might have taken that a bit too sharply. Now, where'd you see the turn?"

"Yes, you should do that more often." I cheered him on, but he appeared more startled than adrenaline-fueled.

"Just up on your left," I said. "It's easy to miss."

We slowed down, and then I spotted a dirt road between lofty pines. "There," I called out, pointing at it.

"Get your hand out of my face so I can see." Then he took the turn, and we were entering a narrow dirt road, the car bouncing beneath us across the gravelly road. "Your suspension's gonna be shot after this ride."

"If we find Alistair, it'll be worth it."

With no clue how long we'd been driving, we finally came out to a clearing with one black SUV parked on an overgrown lawn in front of a run-down derelict house.

"Looks like a hideout spot where shitheads like Alistair would hide." I studied the boarded-up windows, looking like they hadn't been there a long time.

"It's not the kind of location I expected from Alistair after what Rune had told us about him. It sounded like a penthouse was more his style."

"I bet he's not staying long in one place right now, so it makes sense he'd stay where he'd least be expected, right? Besides, this backwater-looking dump feels more up his alley if you ask me."

We parked and climbed out in the fresh breeze.

We'd barely made it a few steps when Alistair himself stepped out from behind the black SUV. Hands deep in his pockets, he strolled casually before us like he'd been waiting for us. None of his minions were in sight, but that meant shit. They would have been watching us from the moment we turned down this road.

The bastard took a step closer then paused. "I was wondering how long it'd take you to track me down. How's my whore of a fated mate doing? I sure hope you're not stretching out her cunt too much... after all, she doesn't belong to you."

"Like fuck she doesn't. She's ours," I snapped.

But to my surprise, it was Wilder who burst forward at full speed, charging for Alistair. Of course, that made me all kinds of excited, and I lunged in right behind him, expecting his wolves to burst out towards us any second now.

My gaze caught the blade in Wilder's fist just as he slammed right into Alistair, and I internally cheered that he'd actually managed to catch him off guard quick enough to kill him.

But instead of seeing the satisfying ache on Alistair's face, Wilder literally bounced off him as if he'd just hit a brick wall.

What the fuck?

Alistair chuckled, and I rushed him, throwing myself into a low skid, whipping right past him then whirling around. I threw my arm around his neck when something knocked into me as though I'd just been punched into every part of my body that touched him.

Thrown backward, I hit the ground and rolled a few times from the force before coming to a stop.

My stomach dipped, and I snarled under my breath, my wolf thrashing inside at me because, somehow, I'd missed. Except, I never miss.

Climbing up on my feet, I looked at Alistair from my angle, where the sun hit him in such a way that I swore I could see his aura. Or whatever the fuck that was...something invisible surrounded him. I blinked, still unable to believe my eyes. Wait, was that the acrid stink of magic I smelled on the air?

Wilder stood feet from him, his face twisted with fury, and he hurled his blade right for Alistair's face. It struck what I assumed was some kind of shield, and rebounded, striking the dusty ground inches from Wilder's feet.

"What the fuck!" he snapped.

"He's got a protective shield," I shouted for Wilder to hear, but it didn't stop me from running up behind Alistair, claws extended. I hit him right in the back, and it would have been the most perfect strike... if I wasn't thrown backward once more.

"Fucking hell!"

Alistair clicked his tongue, looking at me and tapping his temple. "Smart wolf, but save your breath. Your attacks won't help you against fae magic. You thought I'd come unprepared, but I'll give you one chance to prove you're not complete morons. Bring me Rune, then swear allegiance to me, and I'll let you survive." His eyes grew darker, giving us a toothy grin.

Fae magic? Fuck no. I knew we should have murdered Daria long ago.

Wilder's face blanched, knowing too well what this meant. Daria was definitely involved. She was the fae queen, and if anyone offered a wolf such a powerful ability as Alistair displayed, well, she'd be involved.

"Like fuck we are." I squared my shoulders, scowling, while a hungry desperation tore through me, scaling me with rage. He was right there, ready for the butchering, and we couldn't touch him.

"We need to leave," Wilder muttered, sounding slightly panicked.

Alistair kept laughing, strolling toward us, his hands still in the pockets of his pants. That was when I spotted the wolves coming out of the shadows ahead of us. I'd assumed we'd be slightly outnumbered when we'd headed here, but I was counting at least twenty of them.

Wilder grabbed my arm, drawing me back toward his car. "We're leaving now," he grumbled.

I shook his arm off me, ripped in half on the inside.

For so long, I'd wanted to kill Alistair, and now we couldn't. Again. That was doing my head in.

"I'll give you one chance to do the right thing," Alistair called after us. "Bring me Rune. Otherwise, next time we meet, I'll fuck her up so badly you'll wish I killed her, and I'll make you watch every single thing I do to her." He grinned so wickedly that it sent shivers down my spine at his promise of hurting my Rune.

Shuddering with fury, every inch of me screamed that I attack him. Running wasn't a thing I did. But right now, I stood no chance. I could see that. My head swam with the reality that Alistair had made a deal with Daria, and we were beyond outnumbered.

The idiot had no idea that you should never make a deal with the fae though. Fuck him, I hope Daria swallowed him whole, but for now, we had some major issues to sort out.

Wilder dragged me over to his car. "Get the fuck in."

I did just that, holding Alistair's stare, knowing too well he meant every word. Shuddering, the feeling of utter repulsion and hatred towards him darkened my soul.

Wilder threw the gear into reverse and slammed the gas pedal, taking us out of there.

I hated Alistair with every fiber of my being; the agony of leaving him standing and breathing ripped through me. Pain traveled all the way to my soul with every mile we put between us.

He was a monster and had his eyes on the love of my life.

And yet, here we were, running away with our tails between our legs.

Heart lunging in my chest, I curled my fist and slammed it into my passenger window, cracking right through the glass.

I roared, fucking furious.

"Fuck, Daxon. You had to do that?"

But I couldn't find my voice, only the primal animalistic creature prowling inside me, feeling like he was going to tear out of me and return for Alistair.

"This is so fucked up. Alistair's got Daria on his side now. Fuck!" Wilder roared.

And we drove back to town, both of us ready to rip up the world.

12

I strode into the bar, trying to ignore the burn inside of me that told me it had been too long since I'd fed. I'd been holding off as long as I could since Rune had left. Nothing tasted like her, nothing compared. It was like drinking water when you were desperate for wine. It was hard to even stomach the idea of drinking from someone else and forcing their blood down.

I'd have to suck it up and get some blood soon, though. I couldn't afford to weaken in any way, not when I had so much to do, and not when I needed to get back to Rune.

I ignored the two hookers who were on the barstools closest to the door, keeping my eyes purposefully averted as I walked by them. They looked like they wanted to eat me alive. Sorry ladies, you wouldn't survive me.

Pun intended.

There was a rickety wooden stool on the opposite end of the bar, right next to the wall so I could keep everything in my sights but stay out of the way. Perfect.

I slid into the seat, keeping my eye on all the supernatural creatures hanging around. There was a grindle of trolls playing pool across the room. They were in their human form, but trolls were ass ugly and there was nothing they could do to hide that. Warts stuck out all over their skin and their humongous pot bellies hung down from the too-small, soiled shirts they were wearing.

Disgusting creatures.

Some shifty-looking fox shifters were tearing into chunks of meat at a table by the hookers. Their gazes were locked on the girls, and it was clear that as soon as they were done with dinner, they'd be getting their wallets out for some fun.

I shook my head. Vampires as a race were much more genteel than most of the creatures you'd find in a place like this. Since I'd been raised by a hunter, I'd grown up in these kinds of bars as we'd traveled across the country in search of our prey. But I still remembered the elegant parties my parents would host and attend. The vampires parading around the ballrooms with flutes of blood, dressed in their finery. One of the trolls chose that moment to belch loudly, his friends breaking out in laughter like it was the funniest thing they'd ever heard.

I was a long way from the ballrooms of my childhood.

I pushed away the pang of loneliness I felt whenever I thought about what I'd lost. I'd carried the pain inside of me for so long, that I couldn't remember what it felt like to not have it with me. I'd thought I'd feel incomplete forever...and then she'd come along.

The first time I'd seen Rune, something inside of me had recognized her as more than my prey. I'd just been so bent on revenge that I'd been trying to ignore it.

Now I knew what I'd been feeling this whole time. I'd been feeling the missing part of me, the only thing on earth that could complete me. Fate certainly had a wicked sense of humor to match me with the woman I'd spent twenty years hating.

Blood matches were sacred. And not everyone got one. Even if you had one, you might not meet them for thousands of years. My parents had been blood matches. The way they'd looked at each other, I could still see it in my head. I'd never thought in a million years that I would have one.

I was the luckiest bastard alive. And the most undeserving one on the planet. Good thing I'd never cared much about whether I deserved something or not.

I was much more the type to take what I wanted regardless. And Rune was definitely something I was going to take and keep...even if I didn't deserve it.

Besides, Rune needed someone like me. Someone with no moral compass who'd willingly burn the whole world down to protect them without a second thought.

Her alphas thought they were up for the job, but even the blonde one, Daxon, had too much morality to be up for the job.

Only someone with evil in them could do what it takes.

Rune would see that eventually.

She could try all she wanted to deny what was between us, but I'd seen it in her eyes, the way her soul had recognized me. I was willing to do whatever it took to get her heart.

She was fighting a losing battle.

"No," I barked when one of the whores tried to slide into the seat next to me. I slid a knife out of my belt and tapped it against the bar, tempted to slit her throat for interrupting my daydreams about my perfect girl.

Probably wouldn't be worth it though. Her blood would taste like gonorrhea, and even under normal circumstances, when I wasn't craving Rune's blood, I wouldn't be interested in that.

Hard pass.

She sulked and arched her back, trying to showcase her breasts. She had a bit of fae in her, probably thought she was hot shit with her long black hair and her—I whipped my knife in the air and hacked the top of her hair off so she had a long bald spot down the back of her head.

A frightened squeal popped from her lips as her hands went frantically to her hair. My knife was spelled so that not even her little bit of fae blood would be growing that hair back properly.

I smiled at her, making sure my teeth were elongated and threatening.

She jumped out of her chair, sending it toppling to the ground, and ran away as fast as she could.

Excellent.

People were looking at me now. So much for the anonymity I'd been going for, but I guessed some things just couldn't be helped.

The barkeeper who'd been taking his sweet time came running over. "What can I help you with, sir?" he stuttered, keeping his gaze averted from mine like a good little prey.

I inhaled, catching a bit of kelpie in his blood. I'd always enjoyed kelpie as an important food group; maybe his blood would do.

"Whiskey. Neat," I murmured, debating whether I could hold off on feeding for one more day or if I should just get it over with tonight. It would be at least another week before I could take care of the rest of the hunter nests in the area and get rid of the threat to Rune. I just needed to suck it up and have a snack to tide me over.

Kelpies could sense danger, and the bartender's hand

was trembling as he slid my drink over, making sure he kept as far away from my grasp as he could. Good little sheep. I grinned at him and he staggered, my thrall already addling his mind for when I fed later on.

The front door of the bar swung open just then with a bang. I frowned and sat up in my chair as five men came swaggering in. I sniffed the air. Wolf shifters.

Interesting.

They were clearly idiots, thinking they were the biggest baddies in the room because they ambled towards the bar, none of them paying any attention to their surroundings. They clearly thought they were hot shit. The rich, hot shit, not the poor kind. They were dressed like they were headed to the country club. One of them was actually wearing loafers and khakis. I wanted to kick him in the nuts and tear off his head just on principle.

Picking up my drink, I took a long sip, grimacing at the poor quality of the shit whiskey he'd poured me.

Evidently everyone in this bar just really wanted to die.

I pulled out my phone, pressing on the tracker app I had that was keeping a close watch on Rune. When I'd licked up the side of her neck, I'd slipped in an undetectable tracker before healing the wound. She'd never discover it since it was made from nanobot technology and dissolved into her bloodstream, making sure I could track her forever.

My stomach tightened when I saw she was at Daxon's house. I'd much prefer she was at the Inn.

By herself.

The alphas dead in a river somewhere.

I guess I couldn't get that lucky.

I knew Amarok like the back of my hand, thanks to my little trip, and I'd broken into most of the buildings in the town, trying to learn as much as I could about the area while I was there. I knew most of the secrets of Amarok's occupants, including Daxon's little basement habit, and the stalker photos Wilder had of Rune.

Those idiots had better be keeping her safe there while I took care of things on my end. I'd initially been amused at their little attempt to kill me, but it had hurt like a bitch to heal my body while pigs crunched on my bones. And the only reason they were still alive was because Rune was the target I was after and it had been more important to get her where I wanted instead of bothering with them.

But now Rune wasn't just the target; she was my existence, and their only purpose for living was to keep her safe.

That would obviously change after they'd outlived their usefulness—which would be as soon as I got back to her.

"He killed Anjalina last week. They'd been doing some kind of role-play where she pretended to be Rune, and apparently, she hadn't been convincing enough," the khaki-clad guy said.

My ears perked up at the mention of "Rune." Rune wasn't a common name, so I was very interested in why it was coming out of the rich prick's mouth.

"Anjalina? Fuck. I thought she was his favorite," another one of them muttered, sounding worried. "He fucked her almost every day."

"I know he said he wants her alive at all costs, but I say we kill the little bitch. She's no good for him. She's driving him mad and she's not even around."

Little bitch? I took another sip of my drink, making sure to catch every word they said.

"She's back in that town. A day's drive and we could solve all of Alistair's problems."

"Are you sure it wouldn't make him more crazy? She is his fated mate," one of them pointed out.

Khaki Guy shook his head, a scared look in his gaze. "He didn't just kill Anjalina. He ripped her apart into so many pieces that it took the clean-up crew five hours just to pick up all the little bits. None of us are safe while Rune's alive. You remember how crazy he was when he had her. All that stuff he said about Rune being more than what she seemed. His paranoia if she was away from him for more than a few hours." He banged his fist on the bar top, and the bartender, who'd been filling a mug with beer, jumped and splashed the beer all over himself.

Seriously, what was the scared kelpie doing in a place like this? He was like a timid worm. I was surprised his pants were dry and he hadn't wet himself.

"You've heard the rumors though. Everyone who's gone after Rune has disappeared so far. Her alphas are psychopaths."

They were definitely talking about my Rune. They were also idiots. Rune's biggest psychopath was sitting right next to them.

One of the guys grinned and adjusted his dick. This one had a combover so precise I could picture him standing in front of the mirror and pulling one hair over at a time for hours to achieve the look.

How did these tools live with themselves?

"She seems like she has a magic pussy or something, doesn't she? For such a shy creature, she's sure collected quite the fan club."

My glass cracked in my hand with how hard I was clenching it over the fact that this guy had just dared to talk about my blood match's pussy.

"Maybe we should get a taste before we kill her. Just to sample the goods and see if she lives up to the hype."

Honestly, I should win a fucking award for the fact that I hadn't started slaughtering already. That would come, but I needed to hear what else they had to say before I did that.

"She's got to be good, man. Anjalina could suck cock better than any girl I knew. She was literally up for anything. I mean anything. If he's still missing Rune with that," he grinned lecherously, "then I think we all deserve a taste."

The glass disintegrated in my hand, catching their attention. They eyed me for a second distrustfully.

"I'm a bit drunk," I responded with an innocent shrug, injecting a slur into my words.

The bartender paled and went to work on the other side of the bar. He knew I was most definitely not drunk.

Satisfied I was harmless, they went back to their discussion, lowering their voices a bit now though.

"Alistair's planning something big. He met with some powerful fae last week. And when he came back...he was different." The guy who was speaking shivered, fear slicing through his gaze.

Alistair was Rune's ex. I'd heard quite a bit about him from overhearing conversations between Daxon and Wilder while I was sneaking around Amarok. He was getting a bit desperate if he was making alliances with the fae. Those never ended up well. He was a dead man either way, though. Either his deal with the fae would kill him, or I would. Because there was no way that I was allowing Rune's shifter fated mate to stay living.

"What do you mean, different?" the khaki guy asked, his fingers thumping nervously on the counter.

"His dominance level was terrifying, man. It was like he'd been supercharged."

I frowned and tried to think of what kind of spell that would be. It probably would be tasty whatever it was. But there was no way I'd be feeding from that piece of shit. My only goal for Alistair was to get him close to death and then allow Rune to end him once and for all like the warrior goddess she was.

The only thing better than normal Rune was Rune covered in the blood of her enemies. My cock hardened just thinking of her smooth skin coated in blood...and me between her legs, licking it up as it trailed down her body.

"Get me another damn beer," one of them snapped to the bartender, ripping me out of my erotic daydream.

I was going to wait to see if they had any other information to give me, but when they launched into a conversation about everything they were going to do to Rune when they found her, I lost it.

I blinked and then I was on the asshole nearest me, ripping off his head and gulping down the blood that sprayed out.

"Holy fuck," one of them yelled as they tried to scramble out of their chairs. I was faintly aware of screams in other areas of the bar as I lunged at the next one and tore his throat out, moaning when the blood from his carotid artery gushed out onto my face. I shook my head like a dog, bathing in the blood spray. A gun blasted from nearby and heat exploded in my chest as the bullet hit me. I laughed and walked towards the stupid fool who thought a gun could stop me. He fired a few more bullets at my chest, but he might as well have tried to tickle me for the good it did for him. My body pushed out the bullets one by one, and they fell to the ground with a clatter as I walked. The guy's face was a green, putrid color, the stench of his fear catching me in the face.

"Please," he begged like the worm he was. "I have a family."

"Is that so? Does your wife approve of you fucking other women? Oh, excuse me, raping other women?" I grinned, my incisor teeth lengthening even more until they hung past my bottom lip.

"What are you?" he stammered as I lengthened one of my nails into a razor-sharp claw and doodled a smiley face on his forehead. The blood dripped down his face, mingling with his tears and snot. I really needed to stop playing with my food. I was going to spoil it. Eau de snot was near the top of my list of foods I didn't like. And with my list growing of people I needed to take out for Rune, I really needed to stay nourished.

One of the idiots jumped on my back as a troll threw a knife at my head. I caught the knife by the handle and stabbed behind my head viciously so that the knife sunk right into the skull of the guy who'd mistakenly thought I was a good candidate for a game of piggyback. Then I wrenched the knife out and threw it at the troll, impaling him right in the neck. It was okay for me to waste troll blood. That kind of blood happened to be at the very top of the list of foods I didn't eat. It was really awful stuff.

And then there was one.

The last of Alistair's men had slipped in the blood spray and was dragging blood across the floor as he tried to scoot away. He at least had the wits about him to start shifting, but it didn't do him much good. As soon as his mouth lengthened into a snout, I grabbed both jaws and cracked them open, ripping his skull in half.

Hmm. That was kind of a good party trick. I'd never

done that before. I was still hungry, so I scooped him off the ground before all of his blood could run out, and I started to gulp deep mouthfuls of the warm liquid.

When I'd drained him dry, I dropped the guy to the ground and stared around the room. Everyone had fled. It was just me, the dead bodies, and a puddle of blood. One of my favorite ways to spend my time, honestly.

The only thing better would be if Rune was here.

Now that I was extremely full...I decided to take a nap. I always did like to rest after I ate. Hopefully there was a good hotel in this town.

I began to walk towards the door and noticed the kelpie bartender trembling against the wall.

He'd wet himself.

"Grow a pair of balls," I advised him before leaving the bar.

I grinned as I walked out into the night air. Dinner was done. I loved checking off to-dos.

———

There was a hotel in town, and evidently, people didn't approve of patrons covered in blood, so I'd had to use my thrall on all twenty people in the lobby so they didn't run away screaming about vampires or something.

I finally got checked in, and on the way to my room, I got a little nightcap from the luggage guy's throat. Once in my room, I settled onto my bed, checking my tracker app obsessively to see if Rune had done anything. She was still in his house, but so was Aldo again. I realized that when I checked his tracker. I wondered how the two of them were getting along. I knew Aldo would love Rune; after all, he was an extension of myself.

But I wasn't so sure that Rune would like Aldo. I personally thought Aldo was ridiculously adorable, but if I thought about it really hard, I could see how people could possibly have issues with him. The razor-sharp teeth, the humongous size, the red eyes...it could confuse people. For some reason, most people preferred smaller creatures, which wasn't fair. Aldo loved to cuddle, and you could get a lot more warmth from a humongous monster than you could from a small dog.

Aldo had been my pet for the last ten years after I'd found him scrounging around for food in a forest near the Carpathian Mountains, and right now he was currently helping me keep an eye out for Rune in case Tweedle Dum and Tweedle Dee fucked it up.

I probably should have mentioned him to Rune. Even after ten years, he had a bit of trouble with potty training, and she might have noticed that by now. I needed to remember to send a cleaning service to his house.

I watched as she led Aldo out to the front of the house and then as he scampered away back into the forest. He wouldn't go far; he was trained better than that. Although thinking about it, maybe I should have spent more time potty training than some of the other skills I'd taught him.

I refreshed the app again, damn internet, and saw that Rune had gone back to Daxon's bedroom. Grinning, I crawled under my covers and settled in. Once she went to sleep, she was mine again.

Rune was lounging on a couch, completely naked as I painted her on a huge canvas.

"What the fuck," she cried as she came fully into the dream, trying to cover up her breasts and her pussy at the same time with the one small throw pillow on the couch.

"Hello, love," I purred as my gaze devoured her body. Soon

she wouldn't feel the need to cover up around me. Maybe I'd eventually be able to convince her to just walk around naked all the time. She was so fucking beautiful.

"Ares, what the hell is this?" she said adorably, her cheeks flushing when she realized that there was no way to hide herself.

"This is your dream again," I said, looking around the room, interestedly. "Have you watched Titanic recently? I'm pretty sure this is a scene from it."

"Fuck," she murmured, her blush somehow deepening. "It's one of my favorite movies."

"Feel free to use me to act out movie scenes anytime you want," I drawled, examining the way the painting was portraying her dusky pink nipples.

I picked up the paintbrush, dipped it into some red paint, and walked over to her.

"What are you doing?" she squeaked.

"I'm going a bit off script, Dragostea mea," I purred. "But you won't mind that, will you? It's just a dream, after all." I slipped the paintbrush along her skin and dragged it around her nipple with a flourish. "Beautiful."

She squeaked but made no effort to move, her gaze locked on me, her breath coming out in heaving gasps. Keeping my eyes on hers, I slowly circled her other nipple, waiting for her to say something...to tell me to stop.

But she just kept looking at me with those fuck me eyes. My perfect girl.

I dipped the paintbrush in yellow this time and began to trail it down her stomach, where I stopped and circled her belly button.

Using pink this time, I inched towards her pussy. The smell of her weeping cunt was permeating the room. I wasn't a shifter, but her scent made me want to roll around in it, to carry it on my skin always. It was maddening.

She'd smelled amazing before we'd blood-matched, but now...it was mind-blowing.

Her breath hitched thinking I was going to touch her clit, but I had other plans. I wasn't done teasing her, not yet at least.

I dragged the paint down the inside of one thigh and then the other, and she moaned...loudly. Her pupils were blown out, black overtaking everything else as she stared up at me.

"You know who you belong to, don't you, Dragostea mea?" I purred, grabbing a clean paintbrush from the table next to the easel and stroking it through the wet heat of her pussy. Her hips bucked up and she mewed.

"I'm not 'your love'," she told me, but it came out feeble, without any gusto behind it. She was obviously saying it because she thought she was supposed to. And she'd remembered what I'd told her, which meant I was beginning to permeate her waking thoughts as much as I did her dreams.

"I'm afraid you're wrong, sweetheart." I stroked the brush through her pussy again, flipping it around and starting to press the handle into her. Her hand went to her face and she pressed against her mouth, trying to hold in her screams of pleasure.

"Let me hear you. Your screams are mine. Every inch of you is mine," I barked, ripping her hand away.

"Ares," she moaned as I moved the brush in and out while dragging my hand through the paint on her body, spreading it all over her skin.

Suddenly she grabbed my hand that was holding the brush, halting my movements.

"Tell me something real," she said quietly. "My soul tells me you're important, but I don't want this. Make me want this."

I pulled the handle out of her and her teeth clenched as she tried to hold in a moan.

"You've been hurt before," I said, my fingers softly trailing against her skin.

"Yes. By someone who was supposed to be my perfect match; by someone who the Moon Goddess had fated for me." There was a faraway look in her eyes as she spoke, and anguish written across her face. "He almost destroyed me, and I vowed I'd never let fate influence my life again. She shuddered, and briefly flickered in and out.

Fuck, she was beginning to wake up.

I grabbed both of her hands and held them to my chest. "I don't know much about the bond between a fated mate pairing among wolves, but I know that for a blood match pair, there is no betrayal. The type of love you feel for your match rivals all others."

She stopped me. "But doesn't that make you upset that you're being forced to feel this way about me?" she said angrily. "You have no free will." Rune shook her head. "He felt the same way that you claim to when he first met me. It was there in his eyes. And then, all of a sudden, he didn't." She stared up at me through tear-filled eyes.

"I won't ever allow that to happen again. The only love I'll ever believe in is the kind that takes work, the kind of love where you choose for that person to be your everything because of who they are and how they make you feel...not because some mystical force told them you were the one."

I smiled at her. I loved her spirit. I could see it burning in her eyes. It was one of my favorite things about my girl. "The first time I saw you, I felt something. And the blood match obviously hadn't been triggered yet. Every time we talked, I wanted you. Even through my anger and pain, I wanted you. Up until the very end, when you got in that car with me, and I made the biggest mistake of my life, I wanted you. I wanted to choose you even when I hated you, Rune.

Her breath hitched at my words and she studied my face, looking for the lie, the part that was going to screw her over. I let my soul shine through to her. I let her see all the broken parts, all the messy, dirty parts, all the evil parts—and how they all belonged to her.

Rune bit her lip, at war with herself. She thought she loved them. She didn't know how she could love me too.

It was okay. I'd show her how. And I'd show her how I was the choice she should make.

"You still haven't told me who I am," she said, and I smirked, knowing she was trying to change the conversation because I was striking a bit too close to the heart.

And right before I was going to finally tell her my sordid little tale...

She woke up.

And I was alone in my room once again.

13

The room spun with me the moment I woke up, and lying down had the world tilting on its axis.

I pushed myself up to a sitting position, but nothing helped how sick I felt. Something was terribly wrong with me. It seemed to come from deep in my bones— a sickness that crept over me so suddenly, it terrified me.

There was a never-ending pounding in my head.

My attempt to just sit still faded when something warm trickled from my nose. I wiped it with the back of my hand, finding a streak of blood across my skin.

Goddess, what's wrong with me?

Getting to my feet, I stumbled at first, then hurried from my room in Daxon's cabin and into the bathroom. I washed my face and the blood from my nose, then looked up at myself. I gasped at the state I was in.

My hair hung limp around my face, looking flat, as there was no color in my cheeks. I was perfectly fine yesterday, and today I resembled death.

Everything hurt, my muscles cramped up, and I gripped

the sink, staring at the blood dripping onto the white porcelain from my nose.

I trembled, a small whining sound slipping over my throat. I couldn't tell if it was me or my wolf making the noise, because she lingered right below the surface. I sensed the softness of her fur against my insides, her hot breath, and she whined to come out. I wanted to release her, but the more she pressed to escape, the more my body hurt and my nose bled. The curse was blocking her, so why was she pushing me so hard?

You can't come out just yet, please, I whispered to her internally, tensing all over as more blood dripped from my nose. Yet, she kept pressing me as if she had a mind of her own.

Goddess, there was so much blood.

What was wrong with my wolf?

"Rune," Wilder's startled voice broke through my thoughts, and I raised my head to find him standing in the bathroom doorway. A startled look captured his expression, one of horror and trepidation. "You're bleeding."

He rushed into the bathroom, grabbed one of the towels hanging on the rack, and brought it urgently to my nose because the bleeding was growing worse.

"I-I don't know what's going on," I muffled my words against the towel covering my mouth as I tried to wipe the blood. Then I held the blue towel, now blotchy with my blood, against my nose.

"You need to lie down," Wilder told me, and he lifted me off my feet instantly.

I cried out, the room starting to spin wildly, and my eyes were fluttering upward as my stomach turned from the nausea consuming me. "Please, put me down," I pleaded.

"Rune, baby, tell me what's going on. Tell me what to do to fix you." Wilder's voice was drowning in agony.

But all I could do was hold onto his shirt, clinging to him for dear life as my world no longer made sense.

My knees curled under me, and I tucked my head against Wilder's chest—the pain in my head too much, the sickness churning inside me continuing, and the bleeding from my nose refusing to stop.

Wilder drew me closer, holding me tight against him. "Baby, please talk to me so I know how to help you. You're scaring me."

His pleading echoed in my ears, while my wolf's whines were like a blade shredding my heart. She kept pushing and pushing to emerge as if something called to her.

"She's trying to come out," I murmured.

"Who, Rune? Who is?"

I swallowed back the pain and tears. "My wolf. I don't understand what's going on, but I feel like something is forcing her out of me." I drew in raspy breaths, a sharp pain deepening across my middle the harder my wolf attempted to emerge.

On top of that, the towel was soaking with so much of my blood that I was certain I'd pass out soon at this rate.

"Why's this happening to me?" I cried, still in Wilder's arms. The question ricocheted in my head with each thump of my heart. "Why do bad things keep happening to me?"

"Baby, we'll fix this, I promise."

The rest of his words faded behind Daxon's growl as he burst into the room. "I smell blood," he blurted, then rushed over to my side the moment he saw my state.

"What the fuck's going on? Sweetheart, who hurt you?" He dragged me out of Wilder's arms and cradled me in his,

his hand running over my brow. The heartache behind his eyes was touching.

I shuddered in his arms, my breaths becoming raspy.

"Her nose won't stop bleeding," Wilder stated. "She said her wolf is trying to come out on its own."

"How the hell does that happen?" Daxon muttered. "That's not possible." He paused, his brow furrowing, his arms holding me even closer.

Then he took me to the bed and sat me on the edge of the mattress. Wilder darted into the bathroom and returned with a new towel, replacing the bloody one. The moment he did that, a gush of blood poured free down my chin and onto my shirt. I cried out, and Daxon quickly placed the towel to my nose and started to wipe the mess from my clothes.

"It's okay, sweetheart, you'll be okay."

I sat there helplessly as Wilder and Daxon kneeled in front of me, both staring at me with terror in their eyes.

"Okay, so what's causing your wolf to come out?" Daxon asked.

"Did Daria do something to the spell?" I suggested, feeling myself rocking side to side. "It's like something is calling to my wolf to emerge."

"Would that bitch sneak in here to spell her?" Daxon questioned in outrage.

"Yeah, she would," Wilder growled, his shoulders bunching up, a flicker of fear coating his voice.

"I haven't seen her anywhere in town," I said quietly. "She can't put another curse on me without being near me, right?"

"Unless it's an influencing curse," Wilder stated, and he started rushing around the room, madly checking the closet, turning over the dressing table, and even pulling up the rug at the base of my bed. "Fae are vindictive, jealous creatures."

"What's an influencing curse?" I asked, my voice coming out muffled.

"Being influenced by a cursed item."

I blinked at him, trying to comprehend what he was saying. "She put something in my room?" I gasped.

"Perhaps," he answered.

"Well, we did try to kill her," Daxon answered, staring at Wilder. "Then stole you from her, so of course she'd want revenge." He twisted his head to face Wilder. "And great job on having the craziest stalker girlfriend. Next time you sleep with someone, don't pick a fucking fae."

Wilder growled under his breath.

I might have laughed if everything didn't hurt so much. "I don't know. Alistair is just as crazy."

"Well, it's all kinds of fucked up now considering Alistair and Daria have partnered up," Daxon murmured under his breath.

"Wait, what did you just say?" I gasped, my words slow and slightly slurred.

Daxon shook his head, lifting his gaze to me with an expression on his face like he'd said something he shouldn't have. "Nothing you need to worry yourself with right now. We just need you to heal."

Maybe he was right. Except, if he was right, things were about to get a hell of a lot more complicated.

"We need to check everything in her room," Wilder ordered, pawing through my underwear drawer. "Think about it. She cursed Rune to suppress her wolf, so what better way to eliminate our girl than to force her wolf to come out while still cursed?"

I really hated the sound of that. "I don't want to die," I whispered, my voice cracking.

"Rune, sweetheart." Daxon cupped my head and leaned in closer, our foreheads touching. "Don't you dare say that shit. We'll turn this house inside out if that's what it takes." He kissed my brow, and then pulled away.

He and Wilder were a blur of activity as they literally started checking every single inch in the room, throwing things around, opening every drawer, and shoving clothes out of the closet to inspect the inside.

A bone-crushing ache pulsed through me once more, my wolf whining as if she cried in pain. She was suffering right along with me from being trapped, and she was fighting me to push out.

Around me, the room was a flurry of movement from my men turning the place upside down. When they came up empty, they both paused in front of me, heaving for breath.

"Check the bed," Wilder stated as he collected me into his arms, lifting me off my feet.

Daxon ripped the blanket and sheets off, checking every section of the mattress, then he flipped it up and over, to check the underside.

Finding nothing, he pushed the whole bed halfway across the room, the scraping sound against the floorboards lifting the hairs on my arms.

My eyes widened when I noticed a white pouch underneath the bed. My gut tightened. "What the hell is that?"

Wilder set me on my feet and crouched down to grab the object from the floor. It was a small fabric pouch sewn up on all sides. I blinked, trying to make sense of how it got there.

"Have you seen this before?" Wilder asked me as Daxon moved to my side.

I shook my head. "What is it?"

Wilder sniffed the contents and scrunched up his nose at the smell. "Fuck. It stinks and definitely contains a magic I recognize. Daria's."

"Let me see," Daxon ordered, snatching it from his hand, then proceeded to sniff it, having the same reaction.

"Goddamn bitch." Wilder sucked in harsh breaths, while agony kept tearing through me, cutting into me.

A sharp pain lashed deep, and I doubled over, clutching my middle, but Wilder caught me in his arms before I tumbled over.

"We need to destroy the magic now. Fire should work," he commanded Daxon who was already marching out of the room.

"Will that help?" I whimpered, clinging to Wilder because of how hard I quivered. I held the towel pressed against my nose that refused to stop bleeding. "Please let it work because I feel worse."

"It should work. Fuck, it better work. Cursed items don't carry the same impact as spells put directly on a person. Once destroyed, their influence vanishes."

He walked me out of the room, and we found Daxon in the backyard by an old metal barrel.

He dumped the cursed pouch inside, then picked up a metal gasoline can by his feet and poured a splash over the pouch. I watched incredulously as he pulled out a box of matches from his pocket, then lit one up before tossing it inside the barrel.

Boom.

Flames burst outward instantly, a searing heat flaring

over my face. Daxon reeled backward, while I flinched, knocking into Wilder who held me tighter by his side.

Sparks danced outward, growing large, the popping noises starting to sound like fireworks.

I blinked at the blaze licking at the air, crackling. The sparks shot upward, seeming to grow larger.

Drawing in gasping breaths, I stared at the flame that began to take a bluish haze, making it clear we were definitely dealing with magic.

Unexpectedly, it made a loud explosive sound. I flinched with the pressure it caused on my ears.

The explosion seemed to affect my body. An uneasy churning rose from deep in my gut, feeling like it dissected my insides. I cried out, my knees giving out, causing me to fall. The only reason I didn't hit the ground was because Wilder held onto me.

Fear and agony twisted in me, and my wolf winced. The world blotted in and out around me. The smell of the fire awakened a terrible sickness in my belly. Bile hit the back of my throat, bringing up everything in my stomach.

I swung away from Wilder just as I hurled up the contents of my empty stomach onto the grass.

"Let it all out," he cooed, grabbing my hair and pulling it off my face.

Daxon was there too, rubbing my back. "Get all the toxins out of your system, sweetheart."

By the time I stopped throwing up my guts, I straightened and wiped my mouth with the towel. I wiped my nose too, and there was no more blood dripping. My wolf no longer stirred. She sat quietly, almost sleeping within me.

Was I fixed?

"How are you feeling?" Wilder asked. Daxon, on my other

side, still rubbed my back. How in the world did I get so lucky to have these two gorgeous alphas look at me like I was their dream come true when I was covered in blood and puke?

"A lot better, I think. The pain's gone, and my wolf's calmed down. That spell was torture." I wiped some blood off my hands onto the grass. "Being able to breathe easily without pain or my nose bleeding is incredible." I lifted my gaze to the barrel that no longer burned, the thing now sporting huge gaping holes and appearing like it might blow away on the wind like ashes.

"I'm going to fucking kill her," Daxon screamed, to no one in particular, but his hand against me shook. "This shit needs to end now, Wilder. You need to fix this because next time, she might succeed and kill Rune."

Wilder's face blanched, but his shoulders rose, and a furious expression flared over his face. "You think I don't fucking know this?"

"Then do something about it," Daxon barked.

"It's not really his fault," I said, remembering how awful Wilder felt after Daria spelled him.

"Yes, it is," Wilder snarled, the ache in his eyes hurting me as much as it did him. "Her obsession over me is so crazy that it's endangering you. I should have done something about this earlier and put it to an end." The harsh growl in his throat worried me. Then he suddenly said, "Daxon, don't leave Rune out of your sight. I'm going to deal with this once and for all."

He turned on his heels and stormed to the front of the property.

"Wilder, no, please," I cried out, trying to wrench free from Daxon who wasn't releasing me.

But Wilder was gone around the front of the house in a

flash, and the sound of his car's engine roaring only confirmed that he was leaving this very second.

"You need to stop him." I whipped back around to Daxon. "Last time he was next to Daria, she put that damn spell on him and I almost lost him." Just as I finished speaking, he zoomed away from the house. And my stomach sank through me.

"This has been a long time coming," Daxon stated. "He's the one who was an idiot and started a fling with a fae. He has to be the one who ends her."

I blinked away the tears as a horrible feeling came over me. "You didn't have to push him to do it now. Fuck, you could have at least gone with him."

"That's where you're wrong, sweetheart. I'm not leaving your side. One of us will be with you always. For all we know, that could be what Daria wants. And he can look after himself. Trust me, he'll be alright."

I swallowed hard, wanting to cry.

"Let's get you showered and cleaned up." Daxon was holding onto my arm and taking me back inside his cabin, and I really hoped he was right about Wilder.

"What matters is that you're safe for now," Daxon said, but I couldn't get my mind off Wilder.

Please, please, let him be safe, Moon Goddess. I can't take any more chaos in my life.

———

Wilder

I crashed through the fae glamor in the woods with my car, driving like a lunatic.

My pulse hammered in my veins, and I drowned in fury. Rage beat into me at how much I wanted to kill Daria. I'd lived with her shit for so long, and until now, I mostly ignored it. But with Daria's sights locked on Rune, she had to fucking stop.

Madly turning the steering wheel, I skidded to an abrupt stop, the back half of my car sliding sideways, inches from slamming into a tree.

I seethed, not giving a fuck. I killed the engine, grabbed my iron knife from the passenger seat, and climbed out of the car.

My mission was one of urgency and to ensure security for the woman I loved. Rune deserved the world, and I was getting so fucking tired of so many assholes wanting to harm her.

So, the solution was to take a page out of Daxon's book and eliminate the bastards who were making our lives difficult.

With heavy footsteps, I made my way across the foliage-covered woodland to the entrance of the enormous cave. Diamonds on the walls glinted against the sunlight, and I chuckled darkly to myself. Fae were the motherfucking worst kind of predators.

They lured everyone with priceless gifts, shiny gems, and promises of fulfilling any wish. But once you tangled with them, they hooked themselves into your soul and you were forever indebted to them.

I cursed the fact I ever crossed paths with Daria. She'd caused nothing but havoc in my life. But I shook that thought away, knowing I'd be ending it soon.

At the cave's entrance, I sliced my palm with the blade, clenching my jaw at the sting, then slammed my bloody hand up against the invisible wall at the cave's mouth.

I waited. And waited.

Frowning, I lifted my hand and set it back on the wall in

a different spot. Still, nothing happened. No spark of magic, no buzz traveling up my arm. The barrier remained in place. What the hell?

Pacing in front of the cave, I kept trying different spots, leaving bloody handprints in my wake. And still, the cave didn't open up for me. This had never happened before.

I bared my teeth, hissing my frustration, "Fucking hell. Open the fuck up, bitch."

Was it only me she closed the entrance to? Or perhaps she wasn't home. My thoughts flew to Alistair's words about using fae magic to protect himself. Then the spell in Rune's room.

Fuck. Daria had been a busy bitch, hadn't she?

I screamed with rage, going ballistic and slamming my fists into the invisible barrier.

Fuck me...I was starting to turn into Daxon the longer I breathed the same air space as him.

Pulling back, I cracked my neck and thought about my options.

We had to remove Rune's fae curse because it was only a matter of time before Daria pulled another stunt. Of course, the solution was to murder her... along with Alistair. Somehow, Ares had fallen down on my priority list of who I'd kill next. Didn't make him any less deadly, but right now, he was the only one who offered us a possible opportunity out of our shitty situation.

My mind whipped back and forth with everything we'd discovered about Ares' blue stone. He told Rune it would help her remove the fae curse. As much as I fucking hated following his suggestion, we were backed into a corner and had no other option left. My pulse raced wildly at the decision I pondered.

Back in the library, Rune explained that there was a

place in Romania where a royal family lived… the same ones who were associated with the broken artifact Ares gave her. The necklace that was missing its other half that could heal her. That meant we had to take a trip.

It was a stretch, but I was also fucking desperate to protect Rune.

I sprinted to my car. In no time, I was speeding away from the fae's hideaway and back to Amarok. I fumbled with my phone and dialed Daxon's number.

"Is it done?" he answered.

"The three of us are going to the Carpathian Mountains in Romania, so pack your bags."

He scoffed over the phone. "Romania? Is this some kind of joke?" he answered. "What happened with Daria? Why the fuck are we going halfway across the world?"

"Daria wasn't there. The portal entrance was shut and I couldn't get through. Our last option to protect Rune is to find the other half of the blue stone necklace Ares gave her." I hated to explain, but I was also rambling as my pulse was on fire. I had the gas pedal pressed to the metal, flying down the freeway. "Just be ready by the time I get home in a couple of hours."

"You don't think it's better if only one of us goes there, or better yet, send our Betas? It's not like we have time to go jet-setting when we have enemies on our doorsteps. And what if we find nothing in Romania?"

"What do we have to lose? I don't know how else to protect Rune, do you?" I snapped impatiently.

Only his heavy breaths sounded over the phone.

"I thought so," I replied.

"So, what's the plan then?" he groaned. "Just arrive in the country and go hunting for the royal home? The Carpathian Mountains are enormous. We could be there for months. Would it not make more sense to have someone scope out the place first?"

"What the hell is your problem? Since when have you changed your tune from saving Rune?"

"Fuck you, Wilder. This is me being realistic."

I barked out a laugh. "You, Daxon, a realist? Don't fucking kid yourself. Now, unless you have any more excuses, I'll make arrangements with a few locals packs I know there, telling them we're coming, and to get us information on the Atlandia royal family home. We can search there to begin with. I'm not giving up on removing the curse from Rune."

"Never said I didn't want the same." He breathed heavily over the phone, and I could just imagine his nostrils flaring, shoulders broad, and hands fisted at my words. "Fine, we do this then," he snarled and hung up.

Asshole. I had no idea why he was being a prick about this. I would have thought he, of all people, would have jumped at the opportunity to save Rune.

But whatever his problem was, he'd have to get the fuck over it and be ready to face what came our way.

14

"This is luxurious," I almost purred at how special I felt on the private jet Wilder had booked for us. I sank into my leather seat, Wilder sitting along-side me, and our drinks sat on an actual table in front of us. Not those pull-down things. We had a crew of five people looking after our every need, and I couldn't even begin to guess how much hiring a jet would cost.

I'd never left the country before, so I was a little excited.

I stared at the clouds outside the window, and it didn't feel like we were thousands of feet in the air as the ride was so smooth. When I pulled back into my seat, my gaze fell on Daxon who sat across from us, trapped tight in his seat, and his hand gripped the armrests.

"Are you okay, Daxon?" I asked.

"Yep. Absolutely. Anyway, when do the movies start?" He glanced around almost nervously, clearly trying to distract us from how scared he was.

"I never would have guessed that you were afraid of flying," Wilder mused. "Here I thought you were invincible."

Daxon narrowed his eyes, but the moment we bounced lightly from turbulence, fear flared over his face again. His fingers dug into the armrests, and he looked like he might rip the whole thing apart with how hard he held on. A sheen of sweat gleamed across his brow, and he pulled the blind down on his window rapidly before grabbing hold of his chair again.

"I'm not afraid," he rebutted, lifting his chin high, eyes glaring into Wilder. "But does it really make sense to be in a fucking tin box flying? We are completely in the hands of the pilots, having no way to save ourselves if the plane crashes."

Wilder chuckled. "It's a lot more complicated than a tin box, buddy. And if things go sour, we'll use the parachutes the jet provides."

Daxon shifted in his seat uncomfortably. "I'm not made to be in the air like a damn bird. I run through the woods, even swim in the water, but flying, nope. Not for me."

"Good thing we're already halfway there," I said, hoping that would cheer him up, but instead, it caused his face to pale further.

My heart hurt for him because Daxon wasn't a man who did fear. He was the monster others feared in the dark...but I guessed everyone had weaknesses. And in my eyes, it made him real.

Unbuckling my belt, I got out of my seat and climbed over Wilder's outstretched legs, but he grabbed my hips and drew me onto his lap.

"I'd prefer if you sat here for the trip, wearing nothing."

I giggled, lightly aroused at the twitch of his cock in his pants, but with Daxon's growing panic, I pushed away from Wilder. I joined Daxon, taking the empty seat next to him, and curled my legs up as I twisted to face him.

"I'm going to get us some snacks," Wilder stated suddenly, heading to the back of the plane where they kept the bar and kitchen.

"Hey, we're going to be alright," I said, placing my hand over Daxon's and offering him a soft smile. "This is my first time flying overseas, and in truth, I'm nervous too."

"You're doing amazing, sweetheart. I'll be fine once we land."

"Why do you think you're afraid of flying? Or is it heights?" I drew his hand from the armrest and kissed his knuckles softly.

"No idea, though I'd always been told wolves stay on the ground."

"Your parents told you that?" I asked.

He twisted in his seat, struggling slightly with how tightly he had the belt strapped around his middle. "My father. I was young when he lost someone close to him to a plane crash. My father wasn't the most stable alpha, but after he lost his friend, he changed. Then he made me watch all the shows on air crash investigation, making me swear I'd never set foot on a plane. But that was such a fucking long time ago."

I couldn't stop the ache panging in my chest. "I'm so sorry, Daxon. Your dad had some major unresolved issues he pushed on you."

He just nodded, not offering more information. It reminded me of something Miyu had told me about how Daxon's father just disappeared one day. They then found his body in the woods much later, which had been ravaged by bears or some wild animal.

Daxon and I had rarely talked about his family, and it wasn't from a lack of curiosity from me. But I didn't want to bring up what I suspected was a sensitive conversation.

When he was ready, he'd open up and tell me what happened.

I smiled and kept kissing the back of his hand to hopefully bring his mischievous grin back to his mouth, and distract him from his worry.

"Well, tell me, what do you know about Romania? You aren't hiding a secret talent for speaking Romanian, are you? All I know is that it's where the origin of Bram Stoker's Dracula started." If he wouldn't open up, then I'd talk his ear off with nonsense to get him thinking of something other than flying.

His lips pinched to the side. "The country is steeped in lots of mythologies and superstitions." He kept glancing outside the other windows, and each time the plane did a little bounce, he stiffened.

"I was reading up on Romania on the car trip to the airport, and one of their superstitions said if you don't get dressed properly, it's bad luck. So, if you wear one shoe only, then someone in your family will pass away."

Daxon cracked a grin, and I pressed closer to him, glad that this was working. "When does anyone accidentally go out wearing only one shoe?"

I shrugged. "And apparently, if you only wear one sock, then you'll become an orphan. Who comes up with these things?"

"What website were you reading these on? Are you sure it was legit?"

"Hey, it was legit. It was a tourist site. Besides, it said that if any of your feet are itchy, it means you're going to go on a trip. And this morning, my left foot was itchy."

That time Daxon burst out laughing.

"I think my favorite was that if you play with matches,

you will wet the bed overnight. And, well, you did use matches earlier." I wriggled my eyebrows at him.

"Sweetheart, the only reason my bed will be wet is because I've made your pussy drenched with orgasms."

"Well, someone is back to their normal self," Wilder stated, sliding back into his seat across from us. He dumped a bunch of snacks on the table. Packets of potato chips, cookies, nuts, and even pretzels. Daxon watched me.

I couldn't stop the smile that tugged on my lips.

"You're so beautiful," he said. "I appreciate you trying to distract me." He leaned towards me and our lips grazed.

Unable to help myself, I cupped his face with my hands and kissed him back, losing myself to him. My heart raced at how deliciously he tasted, how with a simple kiss, Daxon could turn my world inside out and make me forget all my worries. I wanted to do that for him too.

I pressed against him, relieved to have him no longer freaking out as much about flying.

Wilder's throat clearing had me breaking away from Daxon, and I turned to him, offering him a smile.

"If you keep doing that, I'm introducing you to the mile-high club," Wilder purred.

Of course I knew what that was...who didn't. "Is that meant to be some kind of threat?"

"It's a promise."

Daxon, on the other hand, was still kissing the side of my face as he pushed the middle armrest between us up, then drew me toward him.

"Don't be jealous," Daxon threw at Wilder. "Be happy that she's helping me deal with my fear of flying."

"You're mistaken if you think I care about that. I'm more concerned about how fucking horny you're getting from just a kiss."

"I know exactly how I could completely forget about my fear," Daxon whispered against my lips.

"Yeah, and how's that?" Wilder answered from across the table, stealing my words.

Daxon swept his tongue across my lips, then smirked, before looking over at Wilder. "You can watch."

"Like fuck."

"How about you two sort it out and when you have a plan, you can let me know," I muttered, half exhausted from their bickering, but also forcing them to work it out between them.

So I flopped back into my seat, pulled on the earphones, and grabbed the iPad we were supplied to watch movies.

The guys were talking...more like arguing, but I cranked up the volume to shut them out. I figured it might take a while. On the bright side, Daxon was no longer freaking out each time we hit a pocket of turbulence.

I must have dozed off while watching the movie because I woke up with a startled cry on my lips.

Mostly because I was now lying on my back with both men staring down at me, completely naked.

"Hmm, is this a dream?" I looked around to find myself in the small private jet bedroom. Yep, this plane had everything. But somehow my men had brought me to a bed while I slept. It shouldn't surprise me.

"It can be your wildest dream if you'd like," Wilder murmured, running a tender hand along my cheek.

"That's a bit corny," I answered, but my words came out breathy sounding.

Daxon stood by my side, grinning, looking like his old self again, and I blinked at how gorgeous he was, standing there, groping his dick. Only then did I realize I was completely naked too.

"You stripped me?"

"You fell asleep, sweetheart, before we came to a decision." Daxon's gaze danced across my body. "We were going to wake you up."

Were they? I suspected they intended to surprise wake me up with them fucking me.

I pushed myself up on my elbows and bent my knees, bringing my feet up on the bed. "Okay, so what's the final consensus?"

"You'll see. We came to an agreement," Wilder said huskily. His fingers dipped along the curve of my neck, gliding as soft as a feather across my collarbone, between the valley of my breasts, and lower. He paused just above my mound, my breath caught in my lungs.

Arousal danced between my legs, my body thrumming with how quickly a single touch had me falling under their command.

"You respond so beautifully to my touch," he moaned, and the sounds he made had my body covered in excited goosebumps. "Now open up for me."

My body wasn't my own, because I obeyed instantly, all the while Daxon moved in closer to my side, his cock huge and erect. Goddess, he got that hard just by looking at me naked. His reaction was a huge compliment.

Wilder widened my legs and growled the most delicious sound. "You're already wet for me."

I lost the ability to respond when he expertly slid open my pussy lips and found my clit, rubbing it. Arching my back, I cried out with how quickly desire flared between my legs. Daxon didn't help in the slightest when he leaned over and pinched my nipples between his thumb and forefinger. He applied just the right amount of pressure that it hurt with unbearable pleasure.

It didn't take long for Wilder to lower two fingers across my slick and press deep inside me. There was nothing slow about the way he fingered me, and only when he squeezed in a third finger did I cry out from him spreading me wide.

"Oh, god, yes!"

"Look at your pretty pink pussy, sucking down on my fingers," Wilder growled.

My hips were bucking up against each slap the harder he worked into me. Of course, that was the moment Daxon shifted, bringing his cock right to my face.

"We're going to both flood you with our cum," Daxon told me, his eyes glazed over already. "I want you to swallow every last drop I give you."

"Please, yes," I moaned, reaching out for his rock-hard steel. Burning hot to the touch, it was getting hard to concentrate on anything but the huge cock in my face and the fever with which Wilder fingered me.

I twisted toward Daxon's cock just as he tucked a pillow under my head for my comfort. Unceremoniously, I thrust his heavy cock into my mouth, taking him deeper, deeper.

Daxon hissed between clenched teeth, his hand playing with my breasts as he began thrusting into my mouth, my head forced back into the pillow.

"You're soaked," Wilder said, his voice dark and raspy. He removed his fingers, and I moaned with my protest.

"Think she wants your dick in her," Daxon groaned.

I made an approving sound while working Daxon's cock deeper, hitting the back of my throat. I'd been getting so used to sucking their huge erections, that my throat almost instantly accommodated for their size.

That was when I felt Wilder's cock press at my entrance, and I moaned, craving him feeling me. He took me by force, thrusting in completely to the hilt.

My two alphas fucked me, and it was absolute bliss.

The combination of both men bringing me to a completely frenzied state had me moaning louder. They made me breathless.

Their hands were all over me, and my senses were burning up with lust.

"I can't tell you how horny I am, watching you being fucked by two cocks," Daxon growled, sliding in and out of my mouth, while his wicked fingers tugged my hard nipples. I had my hand on his balls, gently stroking them, and I loved how his breaths escalated.

"You should see the view from my end," Wilder said. "Your pussy is like a vice, squeezing me so hard. I see it clenching onto my dick, sucking down on it. Fuck, baby."

I spread myself wider, my body humming. And the moment Wilder pinched my clit, I completely lost myself to the building orgasm. My body squeezed Wilder's girth, and he roared.

Daxon made beautiful sexy sounds too, when he growled, "Fuck, I can't hold back any longer."

Something that tipped Wilder over the edge of climax as well.

I bucked, my body engulfed by the most incredible climax. If I didn't have a full mouth, I'd have screamed my orgasm. Wilder slammed into me, his cock pulsing inside me. Daxon lost his fight and flooded me with cum.

I greedily swallowed Daxon's cum, working my throat to take it all down, completely losing any control I had over myself. I'd somehow morphed into a sex siren, starved for my men, unable to get enough.

When they drew out of me, I lay on the bed exhausted, my muscles still trembling from how hard I came.

"Stay right there," Wilder stated, then vanished into the small bathroom attached to the plane bedroom.

"You were beautiful," Daxon commented, running a thumb over my mouth. "Those lips were made for my cock. You were such a good girl, taking all of me, swallowing it."

"That was so good," I gasped between rushed breaths. As the beautiful afterglow came over me, my body tingled all over, and my muscles relaxed. "I think I could sleep for a week straight." In truth, my mind was still buzzing from how hot that moment had just been.

Wilder returned with a damp towel and started to clean up the mess between my legs, and I smiled at him, absolutely smitten with these two men.

By the time he finished, we all crawled into the bed, me squeezed between them. Somehow, we all managed to fit, and my eyes already fluttered closed. Wilder said something. I didn't hear it. Sleep had already claimed me.

***

The descent with the plane had been smoother than I expected, and after we taxied and parked, we were greeted by a sleek black limousine to pick us up on the tarmac.

We were in Romania, and a giddiness came over me. I had always loved the idea of visiting other countries to explore their cultures and their rich histories. And this was the perfect place to start.

Behind us, the main airport building stood with a huge sign over the windows–Suceava International Airport.

Wilder explained that the city of Suceava was located in the northeastern part of the country–and this was the closest airport to the Carpathian Mountains.

Sunlight beamed overhead as we hurried toward the car.

A man with yellow eyes who smelled earthy and all

wolf, placed our one duffle bag–because we packed light–into the trunk. A second guy stood out of ear-shot from us with Wilder.

While I didn't make a habit of getting into strangers' cars, Wilder and Daxon weren't apprehensive.

Daxon's hand slid across my back as he guided me to the back door. "This way, sweetheart." Just as I climbed inside, I glanced over my shoulder to Wilder exchanging one of those man hugs with the mountain of a man with a black beard.

Daxon got in after me, and I shuffled over as he shut the door behind us.

"Who are those men?"

"The alpha's second in command from the local pack in Suceava. You shouldn't enter another pack's territory without letting them know, which Wilder had done before we left. And they insisted on giving us an escorted ride into the woods."

"Oh. Almost sounds like they don't trust us." I peered through the tinted windows at Wilder, who was in a deep conversation with the two men.

"You're spot on there. I wouldn't trust an unexpected visit to my territory by two alphas either. So, they're taking us around to ensure we aren't here to threaten their pack."

I nodded and nibbled on the corner of my lips, feeling slightly flustered with how fast we were scooped into the limo. "I'm hoping that if we find the second part of the stone, we get a chance to do a bit of sightseeing and try the food here."

He grinned, pushing a lock of hair behind my ear. "I love how inquisitive you are. Let's see how it goes. I promise, eventually things will slow down and I'll be able to show you the world."

Just then, Wilder climbed into the back and sat across from us, while the two men got into the front. Daxon and I both stared at Wilder, waiting for details.

"So?" Daxon asked.

"They're going to drive us into the woods as far as the road will take us," he said, shifting to make himself comfortable as he took off his leather jacket.

"And then what? We hike the rest of the way?" I asked. "I haven't exactly packed any sneakers for the trip."

"They said they made arrangements for us. Romania has some super territorial packs, and the land has been divided evenly among them. Crossing into another's land could spell war, so they'll drop us off at the edge of their jurisdiction."

"And then?" My tone made me sound slightly panicked, and maybe I was, but I wasn't in the mood for any surprises.

"Then, they have spoken to the other pack about our arrival, who have agreed to accept us on their land."

"You're not sounding too convincing," Daxon reiterated exactly my thoughts.

Wilder's lips pinched tight, and he leaned forward, whispering, "We need to be on our guard. They're doing me a favor, but I don't know the other pack."

I swallowed hard, my nerves building at the way he said that.

"Until then, we sit back and enjoy the countryside," Wilder said louder this time and pulled back into his seat.

Unease filled the limo. I laid my head against Daxon's arm, and in minutes, we were heading down a freeway. I kept looking outside, but our trip seemed to skip the city. All that surrounded us were beech trees.

Daxon wrapped his arm around my shoulder, and we

didn't speak much. Mostly because the men in front could hear everything we said. I hated the feeling of heaviness in my bones. At the same time, I was ready to find a solution for my curse.

We had stopped a couple of times on our trip for a bathroom break and to get some food at gas stations we passed. A few had market stalls by the side of the road, where Wilder bought me a bag of ripe cherries and a local delicacy called gogosi, which was basically deep-fried donuts in the shape of round balls and sprinkled with powdered sugar. They were divine.

Wilder and Daxon just watched me eat, practically licking their lips.

"Are you sure you don't want any?" I asked, offering them the paper bag of donuts.

"That's not what I'm in the mood for," Wilder said softly, and the way he stared at my lips told me everything.

Daxon wasn't any better. When I turned to look at him, he licked my mouth. "Delicious."

I laughed at them and how sex-starved they were, even after the amazing sex in the plane. "You didn't get enough?"

Wilder was shaking his head, running his eyes all over me. Daxon, on the other hand, was in my ear, whispering, "I think about making your cunt wet and dripping at least twenty times a day. Maybe more, but I'm certain I've become obsessed with your pussy."

I shivered. The heat he was bringing out of me was unbearable.

He chuckled. "You blush beautifully, baby."

For the rest of the trip, I spent it by the window, staring out into the woods, the cars we passed, and the endless farms. There were even farmers slowly making their way down the road on horse carriages filled with mountains of hay.

Something about a simple life sounded appealing to me. Maybe when we weren't running for our lives, we'd be able to travel around the world like Daxon had said. I loved the idea of just doing whatever we felt like without someone chasing after us constantly. It was hard to even imagine after everything we'd experienced. My thoughts briefly turned to Ares, wondering what he was doing, but I quickly pushed them away.

We took a sharp turn that led us directly into the woods. I stiffened, convinced we'd arrive any moment now. I had no idea what to expect, but I was ready for whatever came my way.

My hands grew clammy the longer we drove. With the dense woodland, less sunlight pierced the canopy, and shadows danced in every direction I looked.

Questions milled in my mind, but I didn't want to ask too much considering the wolves at the front would definitely be listening to our conversation.

Finally, we came to a stop, and everyone climbed out. I pushed past the apprehension and got out as well.

I blinked at an old-school wooden carriage drawn by two black mares, waiting for us at least ten feet away.

Sitting up at the front of the carriage was someone in a long black cloak and hood.

Talk about ominous.

"What's that?" Daxon asked, lifting his chin to the vehicle where two black horses dug the earth and neighed. A cold whisper ran through my ears, a whistle that swept through my hair, covering me in shivers.

Turning around on the spot, I saw we were surrounded only by lofty trees with dark bark, shrubs, and more shadows. Hairs on my nape rose with that strange sensation of being watched.

Wilder turned to Daxon and me, saying, "Wait here." He then walked over to the carriage with the two wolves.

"It feels like we're being traded," I whispered.

"I'm sure everything will be alright," Daxon said, taking my hand tightly into his. "And if not, then heads will roll."

I loved his confidence, but with the way he was staring around, his brow furrowed, worried me.

Drawing in a heavy breath, I looked over to Wilder just as he waved at us to join him. Daxon went to collect our duffle bag from the trunk, then we walked over to the carriage that was pitch black with silvery trim around the edges. Wolf motifs curled along the top paneling and the side door.

My thoughts flew to a hearse instantly. The horses' exhales misted into the air. Was it weird that it suddenly felt colder standing over here compared to where the car was parked?

Panic gripped my insides, while Wilder and Daxon were chatting. The whole time, I stared at the caped man who moved to open the carriage door for me.

He was tall, silvery hair sitting messily around his long face from inside the hood. He looked like he could be in his seventies, but strong as a lion.

"Quickly, we don't have much time," he told me, offering me an open-toothed grin. He glanced over his shoulder and into the woods constantly, which left me uneasy. Was there something in the woods that we should be worried about?

Regardless, I hurried into the carriage, with Daxon and Wilder right on my heels. And in moments, we were off, moving at super speed. Well, it was a lot faster than I expected.

A lantern hung from the opposite door, swinging wildly from how fast we moved, all of us jostling about in our seats. "Why does it feel like we've just stepped back in time?"

I gripped the door handle to stop myself from falling over.

Wilder was at my side, his arm around my waist, holding me in place, while Daxon took up most of the seat in front of us.

"The pack who live here don't like to associate with outsiders. They do things old school and mostly live off the grid," Wilder explained.

I rubbed the chill from my arms, and my breath now floated in front of my face.

"Why are we in such a rush? The driver seems to be afraid of something too."

"We just stick to the plan," Daxon murmured.

"And what's that? Is the driver going to go around in circles until we find the royal family home?" I kept staring outside the window, convinced something was running alongside us deep in the woods.

I really was hating this place already.

"The local pack of the Atlandia royal family know where the family castle is. It's been abandoned for close to two decades, and they've unlocked the doors for us."

I scanned the woodland again where the landscape blurred. We moved fast, and we jostled from every rock and hole we passed over.

Wilder sat back without a word, but the corners around his mouth were pulled tight. He knew something was up but wasn't saying anything to probably keep from scaring me.

Well, too late for that.

"On the bright side, there's no need to track through these woods on our own," Daxon explained, clearly taking the same tone as Wilder.

I eyed them carefully. "I know what you're both doing."

"Yeah, and what's that?" Wilder asked.

"You two agreed to play down the danger and not tell me everything that's going on."

"Told you she'd work it out," Daxon blurted, and my eyes grew wider.

"Wow. You were hiding information from me?"

And right at that moment, the carriage came to an abrupt stop, throwing me forward and right into Daxon's hold.

I yelped, but he wrapped me in his arms. "I got you, sweetheart."

Wilder pushed open the door, staring at something in front of the carriage, then proceeded to hop out.

Instinct had me following him instantly, just as Daxon collected me by the waist and dragged me back inside.

"You're not going anywhere, understand? Stay here, or I'll spank you in the carriage."

"Do you really think that's going to deter me?" I studied him, arching an eyebrow.

"Rune, don't push me because you may not like this spanking. I said I'd protect you, and that means going against what you want too, if needed."

Then he jumped out and shut the door behind him.

Was he kidding?

I pushed myself to the window, my palms flat to the glass in an attempt to see what was going on. I couldn't see a single thing, which had me clenching my teeth. The longer I waited, the more jittery I became.

What was taking so long? Maybe one small peek wouldn't hurt anyone. Holding my breath, I reached for the door handle and pushed it open just a crack.

Peering out revealed nothing. Evidently, whatever was going on was happening at the front of the carriage and completely out of my view. The murmur of voices floated on the breeze, and I jumped out of the carriage before I could talk reason into myself.

After all, I had every right to find out what was going on if my life was in danger, right?

On silent footsteps, I crept along the carriage, pausing just behind the horses. It was close to impossible to see who was there, but when I crouched down, I counted at least a dozen pairs of legs. Okay, so the newcomers were definitely outnumbering us.

"There's only one way you'll leave this land alive, and that's if you hand over the stone," someone with a deep gravelly voice growled.

My mouth fell open, and I pressed my back flat against the carriage as a shiver traveled up my spine.

"We don't have your stone," Wilder responded with a powerful voice. "We were told we could visit the Atlandia family castle without any trouble."

Someone barked a loud laugh that was completely fake. Why do alphas always pretend to laugh? Alistair used to do it all the time too.

"No one enters our land without payment. And I've set your price. Now, stop wasting our time."

The snap of foliage had me jerking my attention to the woods right in front of me, and shock jolted through my body. Standing amongst the trees was a fifteen-foot black bear.

A tremendous snarl erupted from its mouth, spit flying in every direction. Then it stepped out of the woods.

Fuck!

The world swayed as I pictured my own death, shredded to pieces by this creature. I bolted to the front of the carriage with a scream in my throat.

I slammed right into Wilder, who turned and grabbed me into his arms, while I frantically tried to get away from the animal.

"Bear," I blurted, unleashing an ungodly sound, filling with panic just as the animal rounded the front of the horses. While I screamed once more, the horses didn't seem panicked at all...it was strange the things that went through my mind when my life flashed before my eyes.

A loud gasp came from the men at my back.

But I only had eyes for the bear. "It's coming for me," I cried out.

"Rune, calm down," Daxon said, and Wilder held onto me, but I shook too hard, staring at the bear who suddenly fell to his knees beside us.

I did a double-take, staring incredulously at the enormous bear seeming to bow down at our feet.

"What..."

"Rune, are you okay?" Wilder asked.

That was when I turned around and really took in my surroundings. Nine men knelt before us, all of them bowing forward, chanting something I couldn't hear at first. Mostly because my heartbeat was thundering in my ears.

"W-what's going on?" I exchanged confused stares with Wilder and Daxon.

I couldn't understand what they were saying. Were they

speaking Romanian? Or perhaps not because even the carriage driver appeared confused.

I blinked at him, and the frustration clawed at my chest. "Do you know what they're doing?"

"Bear shifters are bat-shit crazy, and that's why they live in the darkest parts of the woods alone," he answered. "I'm half bear, half wolf, and that's the only reason they tolerate me. But I have seen this before."

My shoulders reared back, and I kept shaking my head, yet Ares' words came to mind when he called me Highness. "This is a huge mistake." My lungs expanded as I sucked in a hard breath.

The older man stared into my eyes, awe in his gaze. "Bear shifters have been serving the Atlandia dynasty from the beginning. They're bound to the royal line by blood and in servitude. They've been waiting for their return. We all have."

"All of these men are bear shifters too?" I asked, waving my hand at the group around us.

He nodded.

I turned to Wilder and Daxon, who were especially quiet. "Did you know this?"

"We knew about the local pack being bear shifters," Wilder admitted. "But not this." His attention fell on the men seeming to worship me. "We need to keep going."

"You don't think this is worth investigating?" Daxon asked. "Why the fuck are these grizzly shifters praying at Rune's feet?"

"We should leave now," Wilder stated, ignoring Daxon's questions, a sliver of panic behind his voice.

My thoughts reeled, nothing was making sense. Trepidation licked the length of my spine.

The worshiping men refused to get up. Daxon took my hand, and we moved quickly back into the carriage.

"Okay, that's really strange," I muttered. "Is there something else you should tell me about this place?"

"This is so fucking confusing," Daxon said, staring out the window as we started to move. The bear shifters had moved to the side of the dirt road, still kneeling forward, arms stretched out forward, definitely worshiping me. Goddess, this couldn't be right.

"I'm completely lost for words," Wilder said, gathering me to sit on his lap like he suddenly feared losing me. That didn't exactly instill me with confidence. Daxon sat in front of us.

"Okay, what the fuck just happened? One second, they were ready to slaughter us for Ares' necklace, then they were praying to Rune."

"I don't think–"

"Baby, they were worshiping you. The moment you showed up, they fell to their knees instantly like they recognized you."

I had no idea what to say. When I tried to put it all together in my mind, including the things Ares had told me...the visions. As much as I hated to admit it, everything pointed to the fact that everything Ares said might be real.

I curled into Wilder's arms, tucking my head against the curve of his neck. "I'm not sure I'm ready for this."

"Whatever it is, we'll face it together." Wilder and Daxon held onto me, and we stayed that way for the rest of the trip.

When we came to a stop again, my heart was beating furiously. And this time, when we stepped out of the carriage, we weren't greeted by bear shifters, but something a lot more extraordinary.

A medieval-style castle in the middle of the woods.

"Wow." My gaze slid over the enormous structure that must have once been surrounded by a lofty stone wall. All that remained of it were broken stones. The building itself didn't fare any better. There were gaping holes in the walls, ivy growing up the side wall, while moss covered half the roof. Two towers flanked the building on either side, and there were at least forty arched windows.

Grass grew wildly across the front set of steps that lead up to the double wooden doors. The closer I got, the more something inside my chest tightened. I couldn't explain it, but a strange sense of déjà vu was hitting me.

The longer I stared at the castle, the more I imagined how beautiful this place might have once looked. Manicured shrubs, beds of flowers, flowing fountains. Now, the castle looked like it belonged in an apocalypse movie.

"This would have once been spectacular," Wilder murmured, walking across the overgrown grass.

"They were probably all pretentious assholes dressed up in frilly clothes, pretending to give a shit about their people." Daxon kicked a stone, tossing it into a fallen wall.

A breeze blew past, pushing at my back, almost as if encouraging me closer to the castle.

We stepped up to the front door, and the moment I reached the landing, my vision blurred so fast that my world spun. Then it swallowed me.

The axe sliced right through my father's neck.

I screamed, backpedaling and smacking right into the wall.

My sobs grew louder, and I grabbed the first thing I could reach for on the dresser. A porcelain statue of a miniature wolf. The same one Father had given me for my birthday two weeks ago. He promised me that when I grew older, I would become a powerful and special wolf.

But now, I was crying as his body slumped on the floor, blood pouring from his neck. So much blood, that I screamed again.

Men I didn't know had burst into our home, and they were killing us. Killing my family.

The enormous man lifted his bald head in my direction, his eyes smiling as he raised his bloody axe and pointed it at me. "Your turn, little one."

I cried out, and darted from the room, unsure where to go. What to do?

"Mommy," I cried as I sprinted down the long hallway, my footfalls pounding the floor.

Screams came from everywhere, servants running for their lives. I gripped the wolf statue in my hand, squeezing it.

Heavy footfalls smacked the floorboards behind me, and I screamed with terror as my skin pricked with fear.

I threw myself down the stairs, practically leaping them in a few jumps, just as I'd do most mornings and be screamed at for doing so by my mother.

Frantically, I swung to the right and darted toward the kitchens when Mama appeared from a room.

"With me," she cried out, her hands grabbing me by my arm and hauling me away. "You need to get out of here, okay? Don't be scared."

But those footfalls still came for me, and when I looked back, the huge monstrous man barrelled down on us.

I screamed, and then everything happened too fast.

"Run, my little wolf, run," Mama's voice croaked.

She then looked over my shoulder at someone and said to them, "Take her now." Then my mother shoved me forward, while she fell back. She lifted a vase and threw it at the man. But he was on her in seconds, slamming into her so hard, I heard the snap of her spine.

"Mommy," I cried, my knees buckling, my heart shattering.

Just as the man looked at me, making a tsking sound, three other guards rushed into the castle and jumped on him.

That was when someone else grabbed my arm from behind.

I screamed and thrashed against them.

"Hush, little one. You're safe with me, but we need to go now. I'm your mom's friend." She grasped my hand, squeezing it, and dragged me toward the basement door in a mad flurry.

I kept looking back at my mama, lying on the floor in a heap, her eyes open...dead.

Sobs choked me just as I turned back towards the woman who had a hold of me, shoving us both through the basement door. And when I looked up to see who she was, I gasped.

I'd never seen her before... but I knew her...

15

RUNE

I stumbled as I came out of the vision, the switch back to the present jarring to my sense of equilibrium.

What the fuck had just happened?

Daxon caught me around the waist right before I face-planted onto the hard stone floor.

"You alright, baby?" Daxon asked. I was trembling in his arms, and he held me tighter against him, searching my face.

"Are you feeling sick again? Do we need to stop?" Wilder pressed anxiously.

I shook my head, taking a deep breath and looking up at the castle doorway and then behind us to the gloomy sky.

I could have sworn it had been perfectly sunny on the way here, and now it looked like the clouds were going to drop buckets of rain on us any minute. A gust of wind blew by, scattering leaves across the pathway in front of us, and I shivered, wishing I had a thicker coat on.

"I saw something. Some kind of vision," I began slowly, staring up at the large wooden door in front of us. "I've been here before. I swear I have." My voice drifted off on a whisper as a crow flew past, squawking loudly. "We're supposed to be here right now. I can feel it."

"Visions are never good in my experience," growled Daxon in frustration, looking like he wanted to drag me away from the place. I pushed away from his chest, determined to fight this out if he tried to get us to leave. He brushed his hair out of his face and gritted his teeth, staring up at the sky for a long minute before he looked back at me. "If anything weird happens in there, tell me you'll listen to me and we'll leave immediately," he ordered.

I bit my lip. "Define weird," I retorted, thinking that my whole life was basically just one weird thing after another. I wouldn't do anything if I had to leave every time something else happened.

Wilder chuckled next to me and I grinned, doing my best to push the anxious feelings from the vision away.

"You're supposed to be on my fucking side," huffed Daxon as he shook his head and pulled on the huge door handle that led into the castle.

"I'm not sure what would have given you that idea," murmured Wilder, and Daxon shot him a dark look, cursing things under his breath.

The door hinges creaked and whined as Daxon heaved one of the doors open. Those nervous feelings came right back as I saw the dimly lit foyer in front of us. It was at least three stories tall with a rounded ceiling painted all over in renaissance type pictures. An imperial staircase stretched out in front of us with flights of stairs on each side of the room, and a larger, grander flight of stairs directly in front of us. It was like it had been frozen in time. There were still carpets on the ornate tile floor, lamps sitting on elegantly carved tables, high backed chairs with pillows askew like someone had just gotten up from them. The air was stale and too quiet...unnervingly quiet actually, even with the fact that I could tell we were not alone.

This place was filled with ghosts.

In my visions, this place had felt like a home, but there was a darkness here now, an imprint of the evil that had taken place here so long ago.

I'd read a book once that talked about energy levels detected in places where deaths had occurred. The author had discussed how the landmarks vibrated on a different frequency than they had before the deaths. I could understand that concept now.

As if he could read my mind, Wilder grabbed my hand.

"I'm telling you right now, this is a bad idea," complained Daxon as we walked further into the foyer, puffs of dust rising into the air with every footstep we took. I ignored him, even though I was beginning to agree with him.

"This place is huge. It would be nice to have some idea of what to look for," I whispered, feeling like if I spoke too loudly, the castle and its spirits wouldn't like it.

"The crypts would be the best place to look if you were searching for family heirloom type stuff, or other valuables," a voice said behind us, and we all jumped, Daxon's claws elongating as we spun around to see who'd just spoken.

It was one of the bear shifters. His attention was focused all on me, which Daxon and Wilder were not big fans of judging by the fact they were crowding against me.

"The crypts?" I asked, my stomach sinking. That sounded like the last place I wanted to find myself in this castle. Why couldn't the family heirlooms be hidden in the kitchen? That sounded like a safe place. Just as I had that thought, a snapshot of the first vision I'd had when I'd touched the necklace hit me. Of me as a little girl running through a kitchen. Maybe I didn't like kitchens that much...

"If you go past that staircase and turn left, you'll find another set of stairs at the end of the hallway that will take you down there."

"Thank you," I said, not sure if he was wanting to come along or not. He nodded and gave a small bow before he retreated back out the front doors.

"For a bear shifter, that guy is quiet," said Daxon, clearly annoyed he'd been able to walk up behind us without us noticing.

Something tugged on my insides, and I looked up the staircase to the second floor, suddenly feeling a desperate desire to go up there.

Hmm, follow the weird prompting or not...

"Let's go upstairs and look around," I said, already striding towards the stairs.

"Upstairs?" Wilder asked, confused.

"I just have a feeling."

Surprisingly, neither of them argued, although Daxon did insist on leading the group up the stairs.

We'd made it halfway up the marble steps when a burst of wind blew through the foyer, knocking the wooden door against the wall with a loud bang that echoed through the whole room.

"This place is fucking creepy," said Daxon.

"You have a torture chamber in your basement. I don't think you can call anything 'creepy', Daxon," drawled Wilder.

"I'd hate to have to push you down the stairs," Daxon answered, flashing his teeth at him.

I giggled and they both looked pleased at the sound,

like that had been their goal when they'd started bickering. Maybe it was.

We'd made it to the top of the stairs, and it was like a rope was pulling me forward, because I knew that we needed to go left. Daxon and Wilder both had flashlights on as we walked down the hall past a row of closed doors that I passed without hesitation. It was the next door I had my eye on.

I stopped in front of it, my heart beating wildly.

"Rune?" Wilder murmured, but I didn't wait to hear what he was going to ask. Instead, I grabbed the doorknob and opened the door.

Cool air hit me in the face as I unsealed the door for the first time in what was obviously many years.

It was a little girl's bedroom. A room fit for a princess.

There was a large canopied, pink bed on one wall, the covers still perfectly made with pillows and stuffed animals arranged artfully on top of it. There was an enormous window right across from the bed with a white tufted window seat embroidered with pink roses and built-in bookcases on either side. On the other side of the bed, there was a dollhouse, a rocking horse, and a table with a china tea set. Everything was covered in a thick layer of dust, and cobwebs were hanging sporadically all around the room.

A tear slid down my cheek as I looked at it. It didn't look familiar to my brain...but it felt familiar.

A breeze blew by my face and I stiffened, because the two large windows in the room were shut.

Wilder and Daxon were both looking at me expectantly...and a little concerned, but I didn't know what to say. I would sound crazy if I told them all the things running through my head.

A mouse scurried across the floor right in front of my

foot, leaving a trail of tiny footsteps in its wake. I watched as it disappeared under a large white dresser with gold fili-gree handles.

There were picture frames on top of the dresser and I walked over to look closer at them. In one of them, there was a picture of a beautiful man and woman, dressed like they were going to a ball–the same couple I'd just seen meet their end in my vision. I traced the woman's face with my finger, trying to see if the picture brought any other images to my mind.

But there was nothing.

"These two were in my vision," I said softly, longing surging through my insides.

"Do you think–" Wilder began before trailing off.

I knew what he was asking. If I thought they could be my parents.

The answer was, I didn't know...but I was definitely starting to have suspicions.

Instead of answering him, I turned my attention to the other pictures. But I was disappointed when there weren't any more pictures of the couple, only landscape shots of the castle, and a few of a white horse. Who didn't look familiar at all. My jaw dropped when I spotted a small wolf sculp-ture on the far side of the dresser.

The same sculpture I'd just seen in my vision.

As if something was controlling me, I reached out and grabbed the wolf, feeling a strange weight on my shoulders until the moment I'd slid it into my pocket.

This place was scary.

"Let's go," I murmured nervously, turning towards the door and flinching when I thought I saw a shadow passing by the door. "Did you see that?" I asked, and Daxon lunged out the door to check it out.

A second later, he was back. "I didn't see anything, and our footprints are the only ones in the hall."

"Probably just this place creeping me out," I said with a frown, looping my arm through Wilder's...just in case.

We walked out to the hallway, but I glanced back into the little girl's room one more time, another tear sliding down my cheek when I did. Sadness pressed on my chest as we walked back down the hall and then the grand staircase.

"Want to look anywhere else?" asked Wilder, but Daxon was already shaking his head.

"Let's not delay the 'crypts' anymore. At least it's still daylight outside. The last thing I want to do is walk through an underground graveyard in the dark."

I was in complete agreement with Daxon on that one.

"Okay," I nodded. He looked shocked by how quickly I agreed, but my insides were churning too much to tease him about it.

We walked past the staircase the bear shifter had pointed to and found ourselves in a long hallway like he'd said. There were no windows in there, and it was testing my nerves to walk down the hall with only flashlights to guide us.

Somehow, the ghosts that I'd seen in Amarok didn't have anything on this centuries-old castle in the terror department.

"I think I've hit my quota for haunted houses for the rest of my life," remarked Daxon as we kept walking down the hallway.

"The psychopath is scared of heights and haunted houses. I'm learning a lot about you on this trip," joked Wilder, but it lacked the usual tone he had when giving Daxon a hard time. Which was understandable. It was hard to feel anything but uneasy as we walked.

Like upstairs, there were doors off this hallway as well, and some of the doors had been left open. It was probably just my imagination, but it felt like there were eyes watching us from the dark interiors of the rooms as we passed by. The guys must've felt it as well, because their steps were hurried. We finally made it to the end of the hall, and there was an opening in front of us revealing a wide set of stone stairs going down. They curved around the corner and out of sight so you couldn't see where they ended.

"I hate basements," groaned Wilder.

"This isn't a basement, you peasant. It's a crypt," said Daxon in a fake British accent. I shook my head as Daxon ducked, barely missing being clocked in the face by an annoyed Wilder.

"You both are ridiculous," I muttered as I tried to get a handle on the millions of bees that seemed to have taken up residence in my stomach.

There were torches lined up on the wall. Evidently, electricity hadn't been added to this area of the castle as I didn't see any sign of the light bulbs that had been in the other areas we'd walked through.

Daxon grabbed one of the torches off the wall and pulled a lighter out of his pocket. "This will give us a lot better light than these measly flashlights," he said as he held the small flame to the torch.

The torch immediately caught on fire, indeed casting a much wider ring of light than the flashlights had. The place already looked far friendlier with it lit.

We began to walk down the stairs.

Wilder tried to tell more jokes as we walked, but our surroundings were too heavy for me to even try and fake a laugh.

The air grew colder as we descended. And

somehow it got quieter too, like maybe the ghosts on the other levels didn't dare come down here out of respect for the dead who were buried below us. Which I knew sounded absolutely crazy, but these were the kind of thoughts that were going through my head as we walked.

Finally, we got to the bottom of the staircase. It opened up into a large room around two stories tall. There were stone sarcophaguses lined up in a row on each side of the room. Statues of people were carved on the top of them, I assumed depicting the living version of whatever soul was stored inside.

On the far side of the room, three coffins were laid out on a pedestal that overlooked the room. Unlike all the other sarcophaguses, these were made of glass, and my heart started pumping wildly as I slowly walked towards them, feeling that same tugging sensation inside of me that I'd felt upstairs.

I gasped when I reached the coffins and saw the almost perfectly preserved occupants inside of them. It was the man and woman from the pictures in the little girl's room. They were dressed in similar finery to how they'd been dressed in the pictures, but there were crowns on each of their heads. The only sign that they'd suffered a violent death was the thin line of glue I could see around their necks.

Evidently, the queen had been beheaded as well after she'd been killed.

Something tried to slip into my memory, but every time I tried to grasp onto it...it would fade away.

I shivered and looked at the third coffin, frowning when I saw that it was empty. It only took a second for my heart to start pounding even faster when I remembered that the princess hadn't been found with her dead parents. This coffin must have been meant for her.

Your coffin, a small voice whispered inside of me. I wrapped my arms around myself, rubbing my skin to try and distract my thoughts—terrifying thoughts like, what if I was standing in front of the tombs of my parents, parents I had no memory of beyond crazy visions?

I glanced back at the king and queen, and a glint of blue caught my attention. Leaning closer, I saw there was a chain wrapped around the queen's neck, right under where her throat had been sliced and glued back together. Following the chain down to where it fell under her dress, I saw a very familiar-looking blue stone peeking out from the top part of her neckline.

"Are you seeing what I'm seeing?" Wilder asked.

"You're going to ask me to rob the dead woman, aren't you?" Daxon drawled.

"Not just a dead woman," I said softly, looking down at the woman's still beautiful face. "The dead queen."

Regardless of her relation or lack of relation to me, I'd seen this woman's death. I'd heard her screams echoing in my head. I'd seen the blood pour out of her wounds as she was chased down and brutally murdered. I'd seen the man's death as well.

There weren't words that could describe the fear and anguish they must have felt in their last moments.

"I'm sorry, sweetheart. Sometimes I'm an asshole when I'm nervous," said Daxon contritely. I brushed my lips against his, feeling weird when I realized if I was related to the king and queen, this was the closest I was ever going to get to introducing my boyfriends to them.

That was a strange thought. Maybe the stale air was making me lose my mind.

"We're so close. Let's do this," said Wilder, starting to feel around the edges of the glass. It felt wrong to be doing this, like we were desecrating their graves. But I had to get rid of Daria's spell somehow. And this seemed to be the only option we had.

After a long minute of us all feeling around the coffin to find some sort of way to open it, Wilder found a hidden latch. The glass lid opened with a small gasp, and I trembled as I stared at the queen's corpse. An image of her eyes suddenly opening as we reached down to grab the stone hit me, and I took a step backwards.

"Easy there, sweetheart," Wilder murmured, his eyes glued to the necklace.

"Remind me to mark mortician work off my list of possible occupations," I told him seriously. Daxon had been reaching towards the necklace, but he paused as he snorted at my statement.

I was definitely not joking.

Daxon pulled on the chain gently until it revealed an identical broken blue stone to the one Ares had given me.

"I think this is it," Daxon said excitedly as he worked to get the chain...without dislodging her head. All three of us were holding our breath as he carefully maneuvered the back part of it past her head and the white silk pillow she was laying on.

"Yes," Daxon whooped, doing a fist pump when the necklace and stone were free. His voice echoed around the room, and I flinched, half expecting the dead to all of a sudden wake up with how loud he'd been.

Thankfully, all the sarcophaguses remained shut and I didn't hear anything stirring in their depths.

After Daxon stopped celebrating, he and Wilder began to slide the glass top back on.

"Wait!" I cried suddenly. Daxon had been turned away from me, but at the urgency in my voice, he whirled around with the knife from his belt held out in front of him, scanning the room for danger. "Sorry...I just want to—" I stepped up to the coffin, my hand trembling as I reached out towards the queen. My hand gently grazed her smooth, ice-cold skin. She really did just look like she was sleeping aside from the grey color of her skin.

I held my hand there for a few seconds before yanking it away, my chest tightening. I was seconds away from bursting into tears, but I did my best to hold myself together as they slid the top back on and once again sealed the queen inside.

"Let's get out of here and figure out how to use this stone," Daxon said, sounding much lighter than he had on the trip down here.

I was grateful that neither of them had commented on my strange move, and that neither of them were looking at me like I was crazy.

"Ready to go?" murmured Wilder. I nodded, wanting to get as far away from this place as I could.

I had so many questions about my past, but if this castle was my past...I didn't know that I wanted anything to do with it.

As we walked across the room, more tears fell, but they froze when I felt goosebumps on the back of my neck, like someone was staring directly at it. I moved closer to Daxon and Wilder and glanced over my shoulder, seeing nothing but the outline of the glass coffins fading as the torch moved away and once again left them in darkness.

We'd just made it to the stairs when Daxon suddenly handed the torch to Wilder and darted back to the empty coffin most likely meant for the princess.

In a swift, shocking move, he began to punch the glass, shattering it into a million pieces as he used his claws to slice it up.

A second later, the coffin in a million pieces, he was back standing by us.

"What the fuck was that?" asked Wilder as he put a hand on my lower back and began to hustle me up the stairs like he was afraid that Daxon's craziness was catching.

"If you are the missing princess, I wanted to make sure that coffin was never an option," he growled.

"Oh. Nice move," Wilder replied.

If I was honest with myself, it made me feel a lot better to know that coffin didn't exist either.

We made it back to the top of the stairs, and Daxon kept the torch with us as we headed down the hallway again to get back to the foyer, a feeling of hope threaded between the three of us now that we had the stone.

I'd just stepped into the foyer when I was suddenly yanked out from where I'd been walking in between Daxon and Wilder.

I screeched as I found myself against a hard chest...

"Hello love," said Ares with a naughty grin as he held me tightly. "I told you I'd be back." His lips crashed against mine, his tongue slipping into my mouth as one of his hands slid down my back. A roar sliced through the air right before I was ripped away from his grip and pulled against Daxon's chest, as Wilder crashed into Ares.

They started tearing into each other, and I looked back at Daxon, prepared to ask him to help. Whatever words I'd been about to say caught in my throat when I saw the wild look in Daxon's gaze as he stared down at me possessively.

"Daxon?" I asked, watching as Daxon began to shift into his wolf.

"Mine," he growled in an inhuman voice. And then he was biting down onto my shoulder, power rushing into me as the mating magic tried to take hold.

"Rune, no!" I heard Ares cry.

But it was too late.

Unlike the other times, where the mating bite hadn't taken hold, this time...it did.

Find out what happens to Rune and her men next in Wild Kiss...

When Syn is rejected by her fated mate, she thinks her life is over.

But when a violent stranger arrives in town and sees her, everything changes.

She finds herself at his complete mercy when he steals her away in the middle of the night.

Her captor is a beautiful and cruel man who holds a million secrets behind the mask he shows the world.

And when he takes her to his island compound, and she meets his two brothers...all bets are off.

It's a fight for survival against three alphas who always get their way.

Can Syn find a way to tame both their tempers and their hearts?

Or is she one wrong move away from certain death?

An RH rejected mate book

AUTHOR'S NOTE

I mean that ending...right? I'm thinking this book has definitely gone from menage to RH now...or has it?

The mystery continues.

Rune's world is so much fun to write. Bear shifters, vampires, trolls...I mean anything is game at this point.

That's what makes it fun, right?

Real talk:

This book could not have happened without our tribe. And I literally mean that. As a lot of you know, I was really sick during the winter and my writing schedule went topsy turvy. Thanks to an Amazon glitch, this book had to be finished with a tight deadline, and our betas and editor came through. We're the luckiest authors alive to have a group of people willing to help us at a moment's notice.

*A huge thank you to Janie, Jennifer, Asheley, Maria, and Jacqueline who came running when I called for help and made this book sparkle.

*Another thank you to Leah and Caitlin. I'm so lucky to have you guys in my life. Who know you could meet your besties on the freaking internet? Your help, guidance, and support is absolutely invaluable and I love you both to the moon and back.

*Last but not least, a major thank you to Jasmine, our editor. She took this book by chapters. We literally sent them to her as we finished and she never complained once. You're amazing, woman!

*And of course, a huge thanks to you! We've been on this ride for awhile now and all the love you continue to give this series is awe-inspiring.

Thanks for helping us live our dreams.

XOXO,

Mila and C.R.

ABOUT C.R. JANE

A Texas girl living in Utah now, I'm a wife, mother, lawyer, and now author. My stories have been floating around in my head for years, and it has been a relief to finally get them down on paper. I'm a huge Dallas Cowboys fan and I primarily listen to Beyonce and Taylor Swift...don't lie and say you don't too.

My love of reading started probably when I was three and with a faster than normal ability to read, I've devoured hundreds of thousands of books in my life. It only made sense that I would start to create my own worlds since I was always getting lost in others'.

I like heroines who have to grow in order to become badasses, happy endings, and swoon-worthy, devoted, (and hot) male characters. If this sounds like you, I'm pretty sure we'll be friends.

I'm so glad to have you on my team...check out the links below for ways to hang out with me and more of my books you can read!

www.crjanebooks.com

ABOUT MILA YOUNG

Best-selling author, Mila Young tackles everything with the zeal and bravado of the fairytale heroes she grew up reading about. She slays monsters, real and imaginary, like there's no tomorrow. By day she rocks a keyboard as a marketing extraordinaire. At night she battles with her mighty pen-sword, creating fairytale retellings, and sexy ever after tales. In her spare time, she loves pretending she's a mighty warrior, walks on the beach with her dogs, cuddling up with her cats, and devouring every fantasy tale she can get her pinkies on.

Ready to read more and more from Mila Young? www. subscribepage.com/milayoung

For more information...
milayoungauthor@gmail.com